RETRIBUTION

Rebels Sons MC Book 1

Gracie Williams

Copyright © 2024 Gracie Williams

All rights reserved

The characters and events portrayed in this book are fictitious. Any similarity to real persons, living or dead, is coincidental and not intended by the author.

No part of this book may be reproduced, or stored in a retrieval system, or transmitted in any form or by any means, electronic, mechanical, photocopying, recording, or otherwise, without express written permission of the publisher.

ISBN-13: 9798883676337

Cover design by: Gracie Williams
Library of Congress Control Number: 2018675309
Printed in the United States of America

CONTENTS

Title Page
Copyright
Chapter 1   1
Chapter 2   8
Chapter 3   12
Chapter 4   18
Chapter 5   28
Chapter 6   41
Chapter 7   46
Chapter 8   56
Chapter 9   64
Chapter 10   74
Chapter 11   83
Chapter 12   92
Chapter 13   105
Chapter 14   113
Chapter 15   126
Chapter 16   135
Chapter 17   144
Chapter 18   152
Chapter 19   157

Chapter 20	161
Chapter 21	169
Chapter 22	179
Chapter 23	191
Chapter 24	198
Chapter 25	207
Chapter 26	219
Epilogue	223

A Note To Readers

This book contains mature themes and is intended for those at least 18 years of age. This story includes references to:

Abuse- Physical, sexual, and emotional.

Suicide

Domestic Violence

Human Trafficking

Gun Violence

Kidnapping

Childbirth

Profanity

Violence

CHAPTER 1

Sarah

The morning sun filtered through the sheer curtains, casting a warm glow over our master bedroom. I slowly opened my eyes, wincing as the light hit my face. Every inch of my body ached, throbbing with pain from the previous night's "lesson," Michael gave me.

"Oh god," A whimper escaped my mouth through gritted teeth as I tried to sit up.

With a pained groan, I sat up as gently as I could, trying not to aggravate the bruises that littered my body. Michael's anger and violence towards me has been escalating. I couldn't remember the last time I had gone a week without bearing the marks of his rage.

As I gingerly stood up, I caught a glimpse of myself in the full-length mirror. My once youthful face was now gaunt and hollow, my green eyes dull and lifeless. The scars and bruises on my body told a story of constant fear and suffering. This was my life, trapped in this house with a sadist, who took pleasure in my pain.

I padded softly to the bathroom, wincing at every step I took. The simple act of moving ignited fresh waves of agony. Staring into the mirror, I scarcely recognized the haunted face gazing back at me.

"Oh, Sarah," I murmured sadly to my reflection. "What has he done to you? I don't even know you anymore."

My fingers lightly traced the dark bruises marring my pale skin, as if trying to soothe their ache. Finally alone, I sank to the cold tile floor as gut-wrenching sobs racked my body. Tears that I had been too scared to shed streamed down my face. I wrapped my arms around my stomach, sending up a silent prayer of protection for the life now growing within. The positive pregnancy test yesterday was the catalyst I needed to finally wake me up. The push I needed to try and escape my marriage I'd found myself trapped in.

"It's okay, little one, I'll get us out of here," I whispered to my belly, through my tears.

All these years enduring Michael's abuse, too ashamed to tell anyone, he made me believe I deserved it. I pressed a hand to my stomach, filled with a new sense of determination and purpose as a mother. I could not let this child suffer the same fate. This baby was my responsibility to protect.

Sighing, I splashed the cool water on my face and patted myself dry. I touched the tender bruise on my cheek, Michael's parting gift before leaving on another stakeout.

Wiping my eyes, I search out the one person who had borne witness to my suffering, Anna. She's my one true friend in this hell I live in. Anna is also Michael's sister, and possibly the only person who hates him more than I do.

I could feel the coolness of the tile floor beneath my bare feet as I made my way out of the bathroom. My fingertips grazed the polished wooden banister as I walked towards the staircase.

From my spot on the second-floor landing, I could see Michael's back as he sat at the table, his broad shoulders hunched over his plate. Anna moved about the room, her petite frame a stark contrast to Michael's intimidating presence. I caught a glimpse of Anna's face, her almost blank expression. She always keeps her expressions carefully guarded in Michael's presence. Any little misstep by either of us can set him off.

Michael's tall figure towered over Anna's as he stood from the table, his cold, unfeeling expression a stark contrast to Anna's subtle smile of acknowledgement. Even from upstairs, Michael's voice carried a distinct chill that instantly made my body stiffen.

"Make sure she behaves herself while I'm gone," he ordered Anna harshly.

"Of course, I'll keep an eye on her."

Michael grabbed his holsters and guns before striding out of the kitchen without so much as a glance in my direction. The heavy front door slammed loudly behind him, the echo reverberating through the house. I jumped, my heart racing at the sudden noise. The definitive click of the lock sounded loudly in the silence..

Michael's parting words to Anna kept replaying in my mind, making my anxiety spike. "Make sure she behaves herself while I'm gone." I knew all too well what he meant by that. One wrong move, one minor infraction of Michael's many unspoken rules, would mean the belt when he returned. Michael seemed to take particular pleasure in thrashing me with that damned leather belt, watching me whimper and plead for him to stop. *Sick bastard*

I slowly descended the stairs, cautiously gripping the smooth wooden banister for support. Remembering last night with every painful step. Michael had been particularly brutal last night. He exploded into a violent rage when I told him I had started my period. I knew he would be furious with me but I knew I couldn't tell him the truth. This baby was mine, my secret to keep to save my child.

"Maybe if you weren't such a fat cunt you could give me a son!" Michael growled out as his belt hissed through the air. The sound of the belt across my back was almost drowned out by my screams of agony, as stinging fire spread across my back. "Any common whore could have given me a son by now." Crack. "But no, I had to choose a broken worthless whore." Crack. When Michael was finally done with me, he gripped the back of my hair in his fist to lift my face to his. With his nose almost touching mine, Michael seethed, "You disgust me! A fucking pathetic excuse of a woman." He left our bedroom, slamming the door shut behind him.

I had no idea how long I lay on the floor sobbing, until I finally gathered the strength to slowly pick myself up off the floor and crawl into bed. I was lucky to have escaped with only bruises and welts this time. My back bears the scars of the many times Michael's lashes from his belt had broken the skin.

Making my way into the sun-filled kitchen, I noticed Anna busily loading the last of the breakfast dishes into the dishwasher. The scent of fresh coffee lingered in the air. Anna moved efficiently around the large kitchen island, wiping down the already spotless counters.

Anna turned when she heard me approach, her kind eyes immediately taking in my disheveled, defeated appearance.

Anna's soft features twisted into a horrified expression as I slowly took a seat at the large kitchen table.

"Oh, Sarah," Anna said, her voice full of sympathy as she brought over two steaming mugs of coffee. She set one down in front of me, grasping my hand gently.

I offered a weak smile, desperately grateful for Anna's compassion. As the only witness to my suffering these past years, Anna has become my friend, my family, my confidant, my safe haven in the storm I was constantly surrounded in.

"How bad this time Sarah?" Anna asked tentatively. She sat down beside me, her brow furrowed with concern.

"Bad," I lowered my head in shame, not wanting her to see the tears welling up in my eyes. "But not the worst it's ever been. I just don't know how much more I can take. I have to get out of here Anna. I know I should have listened to you when you told me to leave before, I was just so scared."

Anna enveloped me in a comforting hug as I finally broke down. I sobbed into Anna's shoulder, releasing all the fear and despair that had been building up inside me. Anna rubbed my back soothingly, whispering words of encouragement.

"Sarah..." she said in a hushed whisper in my ear. "There, there, sweet girl," Anna murmured, trying to hold back her own emotions. "Let it all out. I'll be right here, holding you as long as you need me too. Anything you need Sarah. I've told you before, all you have to do is ask, I'm here."

We sat like that for several minutes, Anna patiently holding me tightly as I cried out years of anguish and pain. When my sobs finally subsided into hiccups, Anna handed me a tissue and refilled our coffee mugs. I took a sip, trying to gather my composure. I knew I couldn't waste any more time, Michael would only be gone a few days, and I needed to act fast. I took a deep breath and met Anna's eyes.

"Anna, I'm pregnant," I revealed in a shaky whisper. Anna's eyes went wide for a moment before her expression melted into joyful delight.

"Oh, Sarah! A baby!" Anna exclaimed, fresh tears gathering in her eyes. Then her smile faltered as understanding seemed to dawn on her. "But...with the way Michael is..." I nodded grimly, protectively laying a hand over my stomach.

"I can't let him hurt my baby the way he hurts me, Anna, the way he's hurt you." I said fiercely, steel in my voice. "I have to get away from him, run away or something. But I'm going to need your help. I can't just leave and ask for a divorce, you know how it is. He will kill me before he will ever let me go."

I held Anna's gaze steadily, new resolve burning in my eyes. Anna seemed to study me for a long moment before she took both of my hands in her own.

"I understand," Anna said solemnly. "You know you can trust me, Sarah. I'll do anything within my power to get you away from him, and safe. We'll come up with a plan, and get you and my precious niece or nephew out of here before he gets back."

Overwhelmed with relief, I fell into Anna's arms again. "Oh my god, thank you. You can't know how grateful I am to have you." I whispered through fresh tears. For the first time since entering this sham of a marriage, I felt a glimmer of hope. With Anna's help, maybe I could finally escape Michael's clutches and build a new life for my child. Maybe there could be a light at the end of this long, dark tunnel I had been trapped in for so many years.

I clasped Anna's hand tightly, an unfamiliar sensation of hope and possibility growing warm in my chest. For the first time in forever, I felt eager for what the future might hold.

CHAPTER 2

Sarah

The next morning, I sat at the kitchen island, nervously fiddling with the coffee mug in front of me. The events of the past 24 hours kept replaying in my mind on an endless loop, the positive pregnancy test, Michael's explosive rage, and the realization that I had to escape somehow. The disappointment I felt with myself for not trying to leave sooner, eating away at my insides.

Anna sat across from me . She had warned me not to marry Michael, then after tried pleading with me to leave him. But the shame prevented me from asking for help. Then, it was the fear that kept me there, and knowing I had no one in my corner to help me. So instead, Anna did her best to offer what little comfort she could in private, a kind word, extra makeup to conceal bruises, a strong shoulder to cry on.

Anna patted my hand reassuringly. "Don't worry, we'll figure something out. That asshole won't lay a finger on that little one, ever." I offered a weak but grateful smile in return.

"Thank you, Anna. I honestly don't know what I'd do without you." I absentmindedly stroked my belly, not yet showing signs of the baby inside, tears pricking at the corners of my eyes. "I just can't bear the thought of him hurting my child. You've been witness to the hell I've endured all these years at Michael's hands, what you go through because of him. I won't let an innocent baby suffer the same way, I can't."

Anna nodded solemnly. Michael seemed to take a sick pleasure in tormenting me, playing twisted mind games and leveraging my lack of resources to keep me trapped. The home we shared had become my cage.

"That bastard has done enough harm," Anna agreed. She reached out and gently lifted my chin until our eyes met, wanting her words to sink in. "But not anymore. This ends today. You'll be free of him, I swear it. That little one growing inside you will have the kind of loving home every child deserves."

At that, a spark of defiance flickered inside me. Anna was right, this did end today, one way or another. Come hell or high water, I would be leaving this place. Squaring my shoulders, I sat up straight. "Okay, let's make a plan," I declared, steel edging my voice. "Michael is away on a stakeout for the next few days. So what do you think is my best way out of here?"

Anna pursed her lips thoughtfully as she stirred a generous spoonful of sugar into her own coffee. "Well, it'll have to be something foolproof to throw Michael, and any of the law enforcement connections he has off the scent. Something that will convince him you're truly gone for good, so he won't come looking."

I nodded, my brow furrowed. "Right. It has to be ironclad. Michael has resources everywhere, local police, private investigators, friends at various federal agencies he's met while working for the DEA. He'd turn over every stone until he found me."

"Hmmm..." Anna mused, tapping a manicured nail against her chin. "What if we stage your death, make it look like you took your own life? That would stop Michael from ever coming after you again. Can't chase a ghost, after all."

My eyes widened slightly at the suggestion, it's crazy, but I couldn't deny it had merit. Faking my death just might give me the clean escape I so desperately needed. "That's...that's actually brilliant, Anna. But how do we pull something like that off?"

A sly grin spread across Anna's face. "I've got an idea. We'll drive over to that cliff, the one that's hundreds of feet above the rocks and the ocean. I'll wait in my car while you leave your vehicle right at the cliff's edge with the doors wide open and your belongings laying on the seat. We'll make sure to wipe my fingerprints off everything and remove any trace that I was there too. I'll report finding your note that you will leave at the house to the police the following morning as a distraught, concerned family member. I'm sure by the morning a passerby will notice your car and call it in too. That cliff drops straight down to the ocean, making it plausible that your body could have washed out to sea."

My heart pounded rapidly in my chest. This could work. The precariously perched seaside cliff was certainly a believable spot for a suicide. And Anna's performance would sell the entire ruse. Slowly, hope began blossoming in my heart. This nightmare just might be ending.

"Okay, okay this could really work," I grasped Anna's hand tightly. "But where do I go afterwards? I'll have no car, no money, nothing."

"Don't worry about that," Anna replied with a reassuring pat. "I've got it figured out." She withdrew an envelope from her back pocket and slid it across the counter to me. "Here are bus tickets to North Ridge, Montana. It's a small town on the western side of the state. I also put $2,000 cash in there and the address of a restaurant called The Ridge Tavern. When you get to the restaurant, ask for Sophia. She's an old friend of mine from years back, you can trust her. I called her yesterday after we talked, and she's agreed to give you a job at the Ridge, she's the manager. I wish I could do more, give you more money, but that's all I have."

Tears of gratitude sprang to my eyes as I threw my arms around Anna. "Oh my god, thank you Anna! I don't know how I'll ever repay you for everything you're doing for me. I know how much you are putting yourself in danger by helping me."

Anna shushed me gently, smoothing back my hair. "Girl, you owe me nothing. Just promise me you'll find some peace and happiness out there. Start fresh and make sure you tell my niece or nephew they got the best aunt in the world. Hopefully one day, I can be there with you."

I took a shaky breath as I dabbed at my eyes with a napkin. For the first time in years, real hope had taken root inside me. I would be free of Michael and this prison my marriage had become. My child would grow up surrounded by love, not fear and pain.

"I promise," I whispered.

Then I sat at in my kitchen, with shaking hands, and penned the suicide note that I will leave on my bedroom nightstand.

> *Michael,*
>
> *For years you have abused me, body and soul. The bruises and scars inflicted by your rage have marred my flesh, just as your cruelty has marred my spirit. I cannot take your torment any longer. My only escape from you will be of my own making, ending the misery you revel in inflicting. Joining the crashing waves, adrift in peace at sea.*
>
> *I am finally free of you.*
> *Sarah*

CHAPTER 3

Sarah

The sea cliff loomed before us, waves crashing violently against the jagged rocks hundreds of feet below. I stared down at the frothing water, shadows shifting across the surface as dusk approached. I shuddered. One false step really would mean certain death here.

Anna gave my arm a reassuring squeeze. "It's time. Are you ready?"

I nodded, steeling my nerves. "Ready as I'll ever be."

I had driven out here in Michael's old Jeep, winding along the seaside highway with the windows down and radio blaring. Anna followed behind in her own car. For 60 glorious minutes, I felt lighter than I had in years. No Michael looming over me, no fear of setting him off. Just the open road and the promise of a new life ahead.

Now, standing at the cliff's edge, doubt tried creeping back in. Could I really pull this off?

Leaving everything I'd ever known behind and starting completely fresh? Then I pictured Michael's cold, menacing eyes and cruel smile. I imagined him inflicting such pain on my child. No, there was no going back.

Taking a deep breath, I carefully placed my purse and cell phone on the driver's seat, positioning them just so. I looked over my shoulder to where Anna waited by the rear bumper, giving a subtle nod.

Then, I turned and walked away from the cliff edge, gravel crunching under my feet. Heart pounding wildly, I didn't stop until I reached Anna's car. There, I turned back one last time. The sight of the abandoned Jeep parked just feet from the cliff's edge, doors flung open, lights on, sent a shiver down my spine. After tonight, Sarah Moretti would be no more.

"The bus you need is headed east from the city depot in 45 minutes. We need to get out of here before anyone sees us and make sure you're on that bus. We should move quickly, get in Sarah." Within 30 minutes Anna is dropping me off at the bus station.

Anna and I embraced fiercely. "Be safe," Anna implored, her voice thick with emotion. She pressed the bus tickets and the thick envelope of cash into my hands.

"I will, I promise," I let go of Anna, willing myself not to cry. I owed her so much. "I don't know how to thank you for everything you've done." Anna cupped my face in her hands.

"Your freedom is all the thanks I need. Now go!"

With a final tearful hug, I turned and walked towards my new future. I didn't look back.

The bus rumbled along the open highway, the first rays of morning sun peeking above the horizon. I watched the scenery speeding past my window, the rolling hills and open pastures. I was really doing it, leaving my old life behind for good.

Letting out a long exhale, I tried focusing my restless mind. I placed a protective hand on my soft belly. A small smile crossed my face. Soon it would just be me and this little one, far away from Michael's reach.

Michael. Just thinking his name made my stomach twist into knots. My foolish, naive heart had fallen for his charms once. When we first met, Michael had seemed so nice and caring, swooping into my life right when I needed someone.

Bounced around from home to home all my childhood, I finally thought I had found some stability in my last foster home I was placed in at 16, with Martha and Jim Wilson. Stern but caring, they had taken me in and given me the closest thing to a normal home I had ever known. The day after my high school graduation, the Wilsons sat me down, then told me come August when I turned 18, I would need to move out.

Once I graduated high school and started working, Jim forced me to hand over most of my paycheck every week. Panic washed over me as my birthday grew closer. I managed to stash away a meager $400 from my tips in secret, but not nearly enough for an apartment or car. I searched desperately for additional work but there weren't many places in our small town willing to hire a 17 year old. For the first time, the reality of having literally no one to turn to hit home. I had no idea where I would go when the Wilsons threw me out.

It was during this vulnerable time that Michael first entered my life. I still remember so clearly the afternoon I met him. I was two months away from my 18th birthday. I had stopped at a cafe after my waitressing shift. I sat outside the cafe at a table, searching apartment listings while trying to hold back tears.

A shadow fell over me blocking the sun's rays warming my skin. I looked up into a pair of brilliant blue eyes set in a handsome face. "Rough day sweetheart?" the stranger asked in a rich baritone, his full lips quirked up in a sympathetic smile. "I'm

Michael. Do you mind if I sit with you?"

I had been startled, but offered a small smile in return. "You can sit with me, I'm Sarah." I found myself pouring out my troubles to this stranger, unburdening the fears I had kept bottled up inside. He listened intently, as I explained my situation.

When I finished, Michael reached across the table and grasped my hand. "Don't worry, Sarah. I know that's a really tough situation to be put in. I'd like to help you." he soothed, the warmth of his strong grip comforting.

"You would? How?" I was a little skeptical, why a total stranger would want to help me.

"Well, I'm not exactly sure yet but I'm going to work on it. Regardless of what I find out, I won't let you live on the streets. We will figure something out." He reached up to the collar of his black cotton tee, and pulled on a silver chain around his neck. He carefully pulled it up from under his shirt. He showed me a gold badge hanging from the chain, set inside a black leather holder. "I'm one of the good guys, you can trust me."

"You get that from a cereal box?" I immediately felt awful for the attitude I was giving this guy. His deep laugh put me at ease.

"No sweetheart, not from a cereal box. I earned it with hard work and dedication."

"So you're a cop?" Michael looked at me for a moment, "I am a law enforcement officer, but not in the way you're thinking. I'm a Special Agent with the DEA."

"That sounds important, why would you waste your time helping me?" Michael looked down for a moment before returning his eyes to mine.

"If I'm being completely honest, I walked across the street with every intention of asking a very beautiful girl for her number.

When I came up to your table and you looked up at me, you looked so damn sad. I think I would have done anything to take that sadness away."

I was so desperate for someone to care about me that at that moment, any hesitation I had about trusting him, completely evaporated. "You think I'm beautiful? It doesn't matter, I don't have a phone anyway."

Michael chuckled at me, amused. "Yeah sweetheart, I do. I didn't think you were 17 though when I saw you. I had guessed you were at least 20. I'm 25 so asking for your number now would be inappropriate. I need to get back to work, I was just taking a lunch break. Can you meet me here tomorrow at the same time? I'll let you know what I find out about getting you someplace safe to stay?"

I nodded eagerly, "thank you." I couldn't believe my luck. Michael grabbed a napkin from the dispenser sitting on the table, and quickly scribbled something down.

"This is my number. Find a phone and call me if you ever need help." He slid the napkin across the table in my direction, then stood to leave. On impulse, I quickly got up, and I threw my arms around his broad chest in a fierce hug.

"You're my hero," I declared earnestly, surprised at my own boldness. Michael seemed startled for a split second before letting out another deep laugh and returning the embrace.

"Glad to play the part," he rumbled near my ear. "Find a way to call me tomorrow if you need a ride." With a wink, he turned and sauntered out into the busy street. I watched him go, my dread finally lifting.

Now, looking back years later, I cursed myself for being so naive. If only I had known then what a monster lurked beneath that charming facade. Knowing now, Michael only saw how young and innocent I was that day. He saw I would have no one but him if he inserted himself into my life. I was easy prey, and he was the wolf. A young girl to be molded and shaped into the submissive, obedient wife he wanted, using his fists to do it.

What I thought was the beginning of me gaining some independence, was in reality the end of it. From that day forward, Michael slowly took over my life and before I even realized it, he controlled every aspect of it.

CHAPTER 4

Anna

The sunrise casts a golden glow across the room, its rays filtering in through the curtains and creating patterns on the walls. My modest room is sparsely furnished, with only a bed, dresser, and small desk in the corner. I live in a small studio style apartment in the pool house behind Michael and Sarah's home.

My mind was still spinning from the dramatic events of the night before. Had we really pulled it off? Had Sarah finally escaped the clutches of the Moretti's? That poor girl had endured far too much suffering at Michael's hands.

With heavy limbs, I dragged myself out of bed and shuffled towards the window. As I peered outside, I could see the back of Michael and Sarah's house. Everything is quiet and still in the early morning light. A mix of emotions swirled within me. I'm so sad Sarah is gone, so damn happy for her at the same time. With a shake of my head to clear my thoughts, I turned and made my way to the shower. As the hot water washed over me, I mentally prepared for the challenge ahead, knowing that it wasn't just my life and Sarah's on the line, but that of my niece or nephew too.

Under the steamy spray, my mind drifted back to last night. The expression on Sarah's face as we embraced goodbye, equal parts fear, hope, and gratitude. She was taking a giant leap of faith, leaving everything familiar behind to start fresh in a new place. I prayed my small assistance would be enough to help her land on her feet. That girl deserved a new beginning.

I dressed and made my way over to Sarah's house as I did every morning. It was time to put my plan into motion. My stomach fluttered with a mix of anticipation and anxiety as I ascended the staircase that led to Sarah and Michael's shared master suite. Each step feels heavier than the last.

As I stepped into the bedroom, my eyes were immediately drawn to the nightstand. A single piece of paper lay on top, almost as if it was too precious to touch. My hands trembled slightly as I reached for it, knowing what it contained. The suicide note.

With a trembling hand, I picked up the paper and read Sarah's neat handwriting. Each word seemed to leap off the page, piercing my heart. The pain and suffering she had endured at the hands of her husband were evident in every carefully crafted sentence.

> *"Michael - For years you have abused me, body and soul. The bruises and scars inflicted by your rage have marred my flesh, just as your cruelty has marred my spirit—"*

As I read on, tears pricked at my eyes, blurring the words before me.

Sarah's cries for help echoed in my mind. She had endured things no one should ever have to, we both have. With a deep breath, I steadied myself to begin the performance that I hoped would finally set Sarah free from Michael.

"Oh god, Sarah, no!" I cried out, my voice echoing off the vaulted ceiling. I let the note fall from my fingers, back to the nightstand, as I rushed from the room. At the top of the stairs, I screamed again before half-running, half-stumbling down the hardwood steps. I kept up the panicked act as I made my way to the phone in the kitchen. Unsure if any neighbors were out and about this morning, I needed to make this believable if the neighbors were questioned. Hands still shaking, I dialed 9-1-1, doing my best to sound convincing.

"Hello? Oh god, please help! I just found a note my sister in law wrote. Please send someone quickly, I think she may have hurt herself! 8523 Evergreen Lane." I managed to get out between sobs.

The dispatcher's voice remained calm as she assured me that officers were already en route, but she needed more details. My heart raced as I explained the situation to her. "I come over every morning and have coffee with Sarah. Today she wasn't here, so I searched through the house. I came across a note in Sarah's bedroom. I think it's a suicide note. She isn't here anywhere. Sarah is never gone, she's always home," I sobbed into the phone. "I don't know what could have happened, or what she might have done. She's just gone." Panic and fear crept into every word I spoke. "Please, please hurry!"

My heart was in my throat as I ended the call and turned to face the quiet, pristine kitchen. The next step was even harder, calling Michael directly. My fingers hovered over his contact on my phone, unsure if I could handle the conversation that would follow. My palms were slick with sweat as I finally pressed dial, uncertain of how this would go.

"What is it, Anna?" Michael's annoyed voice came on after two rings. "This better be important."

I took a shaky breath, willing my voice to sound tearful. "Michael, I'm sorry to bother you at work but something has happened. It's S-Sarah..."

I heard him let out an impatient huff. "Well? What about my

wife?"

Here we go, I thought. "She's...Sarah, she's gone, Michael. I just came over to the house to have coffee with her. She isn't here, she's gone. I found a suicide note." I paused to let out a convincing sob. "The police are on their way but I knew you would want to know right away. I just... I can't believe it..."

"Enough!" Michael snapped, cutting me off mid-sentence. "Are you telling me my wife is dead? What exactly did this alleged note say?" His voice had taken on an icy, suspicious edge that sent a chill down my spine.

I licked my lips nervously. "Just that she couldn't take your fights anymore and felt ending her life was the only way out. Oh, Michael, I'm so sorry. I didn't realize things were this bad between you." I waited tensely for his response.

After a weighty pause, Michael said coldly, "I'm returning home now. Touch nothing until I get there." With that, the line went dead.

I release a trembling breath as I place the phone back in my pocket. His doubts only add to my already building nerves. Did I ruin everything already? Please, let him believe that Sarah's death was by her own hand, I silently beg. If Michael even suspects that it was staged, we could both be in grave danger.

I try to calm myself while I wait for the police to arrive, but my thoughts keep turning towards Sarah. Where is she now? Is she safe? Another prayer escapes my lips as I resume pacing. It's out of our hands, it's all up to fate now.

Exactly 27 excruciating minutes later, a police car pulled into the driveway. Taking a deep, steadying breath, I arranged my face into a mask of despair and went to greet them at the front door.

"Officers, thank god you're here," I cried, fresh tears springing to my eyes on command.

"I'm officer Collins," the first officer introduced himself, gesturing towards his female partner. "And this is my partner, officer Kennedy."

"We were dispatched here for a possible suicide." explained officer Kennedy. "Can you tell us what's going on here today ma'am?"

"Yes, of course, if you'll follow me, I can show you the note I found this morning when I went into my sister in law's bedroom." I then led the two grim-faced officers upstairs to the master suite, doing my best impression of a distraught, confused loved one.

I pointed a trembling hand at the nightstand where I had replaced Sarah's suicide note. While officer Kennedy bagged the note, the other gently asked, "Have you noticed anything off or out of the ordinary with Mrs. Moretti lately? Any signs you can think of that might lead you to believe she would harm herself?"

Shaking my head slowly, "Sarah had seemed a little depressed lately, but never suicidal. She is always awake and usually in the kitchen by 7:30 to have coffee with me. She never came down this morning. I assumed she might be feeling under the weather today, or perhaps was just tired and slept in. I expected her to be here when I came into the bedroom, but she wasn't, and I found the note." I explained with tears slowly rolling down my cheeks.

After thoroughly searching the bedroom, the officers asked to look around the rest of the house. Nearly two long, grueling hours had passed since the officers arrived. They scoured every inch of the home, meticulously examining each room and asking me endless questions. My heart raced as I tried to maintain composure and keep my story straight. Finally, they informed me that a detective would be in touch for follow-up questioning. As soon as they left, an overwhelming sense of relief and exhaustion washed over me, like a wave crashing onto the shore. I had done it; I convinced them. Now all that was left was for Michael to believe it too.

My fragile composure shattered as an angry Michael came storming through the front door just minutes after the police left. The sound of him crashing into the foyer nearly made me jump out of my skin. I had hoped for more time before he returned, but it seemed that was not meant to be.

Bracing myself, I stepped into view as he stalked towards me, leather boots pounding against the hardwood floors.

"Where is she, Anna?" he demanded coldly before I could get a word out. His piercing ice-blue eyes bore into me, seeming to detect my deception instantly. "Tell me what really happened here."

I stammered, "I.. I don't know what you mean, Michael," feigning confusion as I stuck to the story I had told the police. But Michael was having none of it. He stepped forward and roughly grabbed my arm in a bruising grip, causing me to cry out in alarm.

"I'm warning you, this will go very poorly for you if you aren't telling me the truth, dear sister." He hissed out through gritted teeth. To punctuate this threat, he violently threw me backwards. I collided painfully with the wall, barely staying on my feet. One hand flew to my throbbing shoulder as a jolt of real fear shot through me.

All traces of the normally charming, polished Michael were gone. This was the dark, dangerous man who had abused and tormented Sarah for so long, and me before her.

"I swear, I don't know anything," I managed to choke out, hot tears streaking down my face. Whether from the pain in my shoulder or fear for my life, I couldn't say. "Please, Michael, I found the note and called the police, and then I called you. That's all there is to tell you. Please, I'd never betray you," I gasped out weakly, my legs threatening to give out.

As if in answer to my prayers, Michael's phone suddenly broke the tense silence. His hand shot to his pocket and retrieved the device, its bright screen illuminating his hardened features as he glared down at it. For a brief moment, his eyes flicked up to me with uncertainty, as if torn between answering the call or continuing grilling me for answers. The moment dragged on as the phone continued to ring, filling the room with an awkward tension, before Michael finally turned his back to me and retreated to his home office. The sound of his heavy footsteps echoed through the empty hallway. Grateful for the temporary reprieve, I decided to clean the house to distract myself.

A few hours passed and it was late in the evening. The doorbell chimed just as I was finishing the laundry. My heart raced as I hurried to answer it. Officer Collins and Officer Kennedy stood at the front door when I opened it with solemn expressions. Michael must have heard them arrive because he appeared next to me in an instant. I jumped, caught off guard by his sudden appearance. His piercing gaze briefly studied my face before shifting his focus to the two officers.

"Agent Moretti? I'm Officer Collins, this is Officer Kennedy. We were the officers that responded to the 9-1-1 call placed from your home early this morning. We have already spoken to your sister, Anna, we would like to speak with you since you are home. We have an update on your wife's case. If you have a moment, we would like to come in and speak with you."

Michael remained impassive, but I sensed his entire body was coiled tight as a spring. This was the moment of truth. Would he buy their account of Sarah's alleged suicide? "Yes, of course." Michael waved his arm, indicating for the two officers to enter the home.

"Right this way." With a shaky voice, I motioned for the officers to follow me into the living room. Nervously, I led them to the couch, where they sat down with stern expressions on their faces. Across from them, Michel settled into a wing back chair, his hands tightly clasped together in his lap.

"Is there anything I can get for you to drink? Coffee, tea, water?" Both officers declined politely.

In a dismissive and icy tone, Micheal said, "Just a coffee for me, Anna. We would like a few moments alone before you come back and interrupt us again." He didn't even bother to look at me as he spoke.

I left the room and turned the corner, quickly flattening myself against the wall to eavesdrop on the conversation. Officer Kennedy coughed uncomfortably.

"I'm afraid we recovered a vehicle matching the description of your Jeep at the Hamilton Beach Cliffs. After running the VIN number, we were able to confirm that the vehicle found at the scene was registered to you, Agent Moretti. Inside the car, we found some personal items including a purse on the driver's seat containing a drivers license belonging to your wife. We also found a cell phone, presumably belonging to your wife. Although we powered it on, there is a lock on the phone preventing us from accessing any information. At this time, no body has been recovered but–".

Michael interrupted her sharply, "There's no body. So she must still be alive." He carefully maintained a controlled tone of voice.

"In circumstances like this, the note is usually our best lead–". Officer Kennedy was unable to finish her sentence as she was cut off once again.

"Yes... Yes, the note." Michael's voice was cool and detached as he dismissed the officers with a wave of his hand. "Thank you for relaying the information. My wife is dead. Now please, do your jobs and find her body." With that, he beckoned for me to come back into the room. "Anna, show our guests out," he commanded.

I complied with his orders and cautiously stepped back into the room. Officer Collins' eyes darted back and forth, between Michael and me, trying to make sense of Michael's behavior. Confusion was written all over his face as he tried to process the situation. Both officers stood from their chairs, preparing to leave.

With a curt nod, Officer Collins addressed Michael, "We will be in touch if we have any further information or need to ask additional questions. Any personal belongings that are recovered will remain in our custody as evidence until the investigation is concluded." The tension in the room was palpable as they exited.

I guided the two officers through the house, and out the front door. As the heavy front door closed behind me, I let out a sigh of relief. He accepted it. We weren't out of the woods yet though.

Forcing a worried expression on my face, I returned to the living room where Michael remained seated. I turned to him; my brows furrowed in concern. "Oh Michael, I'm sorry," I said meekly. "Are you alright?"

Michael stared coldly back at me for several long, tense moments. Then he seemed to snap back into grieving husband mode. "I appreciate your concern, Anna," he replied tonelessly. "I just need some time alone right now to process this. Please go home." And with that, he stood,

turned on his heel and disappeared in the direction of his office, leaving me alone once again.

I leaned my body against the cool, hard wall and exhaled deeply. Being in this situation was like walking on a tightrope, one small misstep, and everything could come crashing down. The police seemed satisfied with my explanation for now, but Michael's doubt was palpable. He wasn't completely convinced Sarah had truly taken her own life. I knew he would continue to search for answers. All I could do now was maintain this exhausting charade and hope Michael doesn't uncover the truth. If he did, neither of us would be safe.

CHAPTER 5

Sarah

The bus barrels down the winding highway, surrounded by towering mountains covered in lush green forests. The landscape moves by in a blur, the trees and cliffs blending together in a swirl of colors.

The bus pulled into the station in North Ridge, Montana, a small town nestled in the mountains. I sat in my seat, watching the other passengers gather their belongings and rush off the bus. This was it. My chance to start a better life for me and my child. But as I looked out at the unfamiliar streets and buildings, doubt crept into my mind.

Could I really do this alone?

I shook off these thoughts and stood up, grabbing my backpack from under the seat. I followed the crowd off the bus and into the congested station. The air was crisp and smelled faintly of pine. People rushed past me, some with purpose while others seemed lost in their own thoughts. Butterflies swarm in my stomach as I take in all of these new sights and sounds.

I spotted a map of North Ridge hanging on the wall near an information desk. I walked over to it, trying to orient myself to my new surroundings. Glancing down at the slip of paper Anna had pressed into my palm before I left Oregon, I made a note of the address. According to the map, it was just a few blocks down from the bus station.

I emerged from the station and stepped onto the main street. It was bordered on either side by shops and cafes, each one beckoning with tempting aromas and colorful displays in their windows. The town was noticeably smaller than the city I was accustomed to, but there was a certain charm to its small-town feel. The buildings were painted in cheerful pastel hues, and flowers spilled from window boxes and hung from lampposts.

After a short walk, I found myself standing in front of a rustic tavern. Its exterior resembled a log cabin, complete with a wide front porch that wrapped around one side of the building. The benches lining the porch were crafted from rough-hewn logs, adding to the rustic charm. Above the entrance, a hand-painted wooden sign displayed the name of the establishment, 'The Ridge Restaurant and Tavern', in elegant, looping script. As I approached, mouth watering aromas and the sound of lively chatter spilled out onto the sidewalk, tempting me inside. The warm and welcoming atmosphere reminded me of a home away from home.

I paused outside the entrance, anxiety creeping back in. After taking a moment to calm my nerves myself, I stepped inside.

The interior of the tavern was warm and inviting, with polished wood and leather furnishings creating a comfortable atmosphere. It was dimly lit, giving off an intimate feel. The walls were made of polished, dark wood, with the occasional mounted deer head adorning the space. The long oak bar stood prominently against the back wall, its shellacked surface gleaming in the soft light. Shelves of liquor bottles lined the top, each one reflecting the light in amber and gold hues.

The handful of lunch patrons barely glanced up from their meals and conversations as I hovered just inside the threshold. Before I could scan the room, a lovely woman with dark, spiraling hair bustled over.

"Hello, welcome to The Ridge," she greeted me with a warm smile. "Please, feel free to take a seat anywhere you'd like. However, if you sit at the bar, you'll probably get served quicker. We're short-staffed right now," explaining with a friendly tone.

I fidgeted nervously, my eyes darting around the space before landing on the woman's friendly face. "Uh, hi. I'm looking for Sophia, the manager."

The woman's smile grew wider. "That would be me. And you are?"

"Oh, sorry! Yes, I'm Sarah. Anna sent me." I managed to give her a timid smile, trying to mask how nervous I was.

The woman's eyes lit up with recognition. "Ah, Sarah, I'm glad you finally made it, I've been looking forward to meeting you since Anna called me a few days ago. Come, sit down and rest for a bit." She led me to a cozy booth tucked away in the corner, where we could talk in private. As we settled into the plush leather seats, Sophia placed a comforting hand on mine.

"It's so good to finally meet you," her eyes filled with kindness. "Anna explained a little bit about your situation. I think she was leaving the rest for you to tell me whenever you feel comfortable enough to." Sophia's voice dropped to a hushed whisper. "Don't you worry honey, you're safe here. I won't ask any questions you don't want to answer." Her kind eyes seemed to understand everything without me needing to say a word. I felt myself relax slightly; my tense muscles slowly uncoiled. Tears were pricking at the back of my eyes, but Sophia's reassuring hand on mine brought me comfort. At that moment, I knew I could trust her and open up about my troubles. Sophia just smiled and squeezed my hand, the gesture speaking volumes more than words ever could.

My words tumbled out of my mouth, hesitant and unsure of where to start. "Anna, she helped me get out, away from my husband. He... he wasn't good to me. He liked to hurt me, badly. I found out I was pregnant and I knew I had to get out. I couldn't let my child live like that."

With a heavy sigh, I forced myself to look up and meet her gaze, bracing for the pity that I knew would follow. But instead, her face transformed into a mask of pure rage, her eyes flashing with fire as she growled, "That bastard. He'll get what's coming to him one day." A surge of gratitude swept through me as I realized the depth of her anger on my behalf. Her rage was a welcoming comfort.

My gaze remained fixed on Sophia as I continued, "Leaving wasn't an option. He would have never stopped searching for me, and eventually he would've found me. I was certain of it."

Torn between whether or not I should continue my story, I inhale deeply before finally blurting out, "I faked my death two days ago, and immediately hopped on a bus to come here."

I am taken aback when Sophia remains unfazed. She doesn't even flinch or hesitate before responding, "You're absolutely right for leaving. I know who your husband and father-in-law are. I'm also aware that in their eyes, if you aren't equipped with a dick at birth, you're not good use for much else besides lying on your back and raising their kids. The legitimate ones that is. I lived in Oregon before moving here. That's my connection to Anna. I left that life behind as soon as I could. Anna... wasn't so lucky. There is a story there I'm sure you don't know about, I'll tell you one day."

My eyes widened with shock, my jaw dropping as Sophia revealed that she knew Michael and his father. A million thoughts raced through my mind as I tried to wrap my head around the connection between them. Sophia's keen gaze caught mine and she must have seen the disbelief etched on my face.

"Don't worry, like I said you're safe here. We take care of our own around here, you'll see. Now, you must be starving. Let me get you something to eat." Before I could even utter a word of protest, she had disappeared into the kitchen. Minutes later, she emerged with a steaming plate of al dente pasta overflowing with savory sauce and topped with fresh herbs and grated cheese. The aroma alone was enough to make my mouth water and my stomach growl.

As I dug hungrily into the hot meal, Sophia laid out the details. "There are two small efficiency apartments on the second floor above the tavern. One unit is mine, the other has been empty for some time now. I've just been using it for storage. If you need a place to stay, we can clear it out. I wouldn't charge you any rent; just give me a few days to clean it up for you. It's been vacant for about 10 years, so I'm not sure if everything still works. I know Anna told you I have a job for you. I'm in desperate need of a waitress. If you're up to working the bar in addition to waitressing, I can give you more hours. I'll pay you in cash every Friday. That way there is no paper trail connecting you to North Ridge, if anyone starts looking. Sound good to you?"

My heart was filled with gratitude as I could barely manage a nod and a choked, "Thank you, that sounds amazing."

Sophia's hand wrapped gently around mine, her touch warm and comforting. "You don't need to thank me, we're helping each other out here," she said softly. "I have to get back behind the bar, come find me if you need anything. Take your time finishing your meal, and I'll come back to clear the table when you're done."

Her words were like a soothing balm, easing any worries or discomfort I had felt before. The buzzing energy of the bustling bar surrounded us, but in that moment, it felt like we were in our own little world, connected by this act of kindness and support. I couldn't help but smile gratefully at Sophia before turning my attention back to the delicious food on my plate.

As I twirled a forkful of spaghetti on my plate, the heavy

wooden door of the tavern swung open with a creak. After a few moments, my attention was drawn to the sound of fast approaching footsteps that stopped abruptly next to my table. Startled, I looked up to see who had arrived so suddenly, causing my fork to pause halfway to my mouth.

The man's tall, muscular frame casts a shadow over me. Tattoos starting at his knuckles and running up both arms until they disappeared under a flannel, the arms rolled up, stopping just below his elbows. He wore a leather kutte, the patch on the front read 'Enforcer'. His rugged features were highlighted by the dim light of the tavern, casting shadows over his face. His untamed, light brown hair was pulled back from his face in a low knot, revealing at least a week's worth of stubble over a strong jawline. He was older, filled out, but it was those piercing stormy gray eyes that held my attention. I couldn't mistake those eyes for anyone else's.

"Jake?" I said his name in disbelief, barely able to register in my mind what I was seeing. His intense gaze never left mine, and I could see the confusion etched on his face. Before either of us could react, Sophia interrupted us.

"Jake, perfect timing! I want to introduce you to our newest waitress." Her smile was warm and encouraging, but Jake's gaze remained fixed on me, almost as if he was trying to read my thoughts.

As Jake slid into the booth opposite of me, his voice was a gravelly mix of surprise and suspicion. "New waitress, huh." His handsome face mirrored his conflicting emotions.

Sophia, unsure of what was happening, gave his shoulder a reassuring pat. "I'll give you two a minute," before she retreated back towards the bar.

A heavy silence fell over the table as I ran my thumb along the beads of condensation on my water glass. I was at a loss for words, unsure how to react after all these years of not seeing

Jake. It felt like a punch to the stomach just being in his presence again.

I forced myself to meet his eyes. "This is...unexpected," I began awkwardly. "Do you live here?" *Of course, he lives here. Why did I ask that?*

Jake's intense gaze made me squirm, feeling incredibly uncomfortable. "Where did you disappear to, Sarah? You were just gone. I thought you knew that I cared about you. You had me believin' you actually gave a damn about me too. I know it was a long time ago, and we were just kids. But all this time I never knew why, Sarah. Fuck. I thought we had something." His tone was harsh and accusing. My stomach twisted with guilt; he was clearly angry with me. How could he be upset when he never replied to any of my letters? It didn't seem fair for him to hold me accountable for something he neglected as well.

"I didn't have a chance to explain everything to you, to say goodbye. When I sent you all those letters, I hoped you'd understand that it wasn't my choice to leave, to leave you." Jake's jaw tensed as he processed my words. After what felt like an eternity, he gave me a sharp nod for me to continue.

I steadied my breathing, determined to keep my emotions in check. In a hushed tone, I recounted the day from fourteen years ago when my caseworker showed up at my foster home for a surprise welfare check. An anonymous call had been made expressing concern about the well-being of the children living there. After inspecting every room, she informed me that I was being moved to a new foster home over a hundred miles away.

"I never wanted to leave Jake," I whispered, tears gathering in my eyes. "You know I didn't have a phone then. I wrote you so many letters, but you never responded. I thought you didn't want me anymore, that I wasn't worth the distance."

I noticed Jake's face change from a stony expression to one of slight softness. His eyes showed a glimmer of the tenderness I once knew. Feeling encouraged, I kept going. "I know you must have been hurt, thinking I just abandoned you. But I fought so hard, Jake. I was only 16, it was out of my control. I went back once to see you, the day I turned 18. No one was home at your house. I went to the bike shop you liked to hang out at. They told me you enlisted. You were already gone." My voice broke as a tear escaped, trailing slowly down my cheek.

Jake's hand twitched where it rested on the table, his fingers curling and uncurling in a restless gesture. I could see the tension in his jaw, the muscles flexing and relaxing as if he were trying to hold back words that needed to be said. He let out a deep sigh, his broad shoulders slumping in defeat, and I knew he was struggling with his emotions. For a moment, we sat in silence, the air thick with unsaid words and unspoken feelings.

"I wish I had known Sarah. I thought... I never got any of the letters. My stepdad must have thrown them out. He was such a worthless fuck. Always had to take away anything that might bring me a little bit of good in my life." Jake said as he shook his head. "You were the only good I had in my life back then. I always hated how you thought so little of yourself. Just so you know, I would have wanted you anyway I could have you. It didn't matter the distance; you were always worth it." He paused letting his words sink in. "Thank you for telling me. I'm just glad to see you're okay."

If he only knew how not okay I actually was.

"So, you're livin' here in North Ridge now?" Jake asks in disbelief. "I can't believe after all this time, you've ended up here in the middle of nowhere Montana, where I am." He leans in closer and asks, "What brought you here?"

I shrug, "I just arrived today on the bus. Needed a change of scenery and decided to leave Oregon. A friend of mine knows Sophia and hooked me up with a job here. Figured it was time for a fresh start.

When did you move here?" I question, wondering how Jake ended up here too.

"I've been here for around 5 years now. Cassandra and Wyatt got sent out here to live with our grandma when I decided to join the Marines, and left for bootcamp. When I got discharged, I decided to move out here too, so I could keep an eye on 'em. You know, keep 'em close. My grandpa, he had already passed before I moved out here. I've gotten the chance to know my grandma pretty well the last few years. I'm really thankful for that, good people."

"That's great Jake, I'm glad that you have some good people in your life now. I know you never really had anyone back then." I smiled, genuinely happy for him.

"No one except you." Jake admitted softly, not making eye contact. Those four words held so much sweetness and pain at the same time. At that moment, I saw the 18-year-old boy that used to walk me home from school, so I wasn't alone. Not the hardened 32-year-old man sitting across from me now.

"I can be again." I spoke without thinking and instantly regretted it. I know nothing about him now. He could be married with 2.5 kids, and a white picket fence for all I know. I quickly added, "As a friend— I mean as a friend." Jake leans back amused, and gives me the sexiest, one-sided smirk I have ever seen.

"Yeah Darlin', I get you. We're BFFs now."

"Smartass," I couldn't help but to giggle as I tossed my napkin across the table at him.

It had been so long; I had forgotten how easy things used to be between us. The initial awkwardness slowly melted away, and we fell back into our old ease with each other.

As we chatted, I couldn't help but study Jake's features. His once boyish face had matured into strong, chiseled angles, yet his eyes still held the same warmth and familiarity that I remembered. And there was one thing that hadn't changed, his love for motorcycles and cars. I found out that he now runs an auto shop on the outskirts of town, specializing in bike repairs and custom builds.

"After I moved out here, I joined the Rebel Sons, and started workin' at the shop," he explained with a proud smile. "The club owns it. I manage it, and do the custom builds. I also do some bounty hunting when they are short handed, at Rigg's Bail and Bounty. My grandpa started that business. Now my uncle Beau runs it."

"That's amazing, Jake. You've really made something of yourself. I'm proud of you. It seems like you're doing well." I told him, genuinely impressed.

I noticed Jake's eyes briefly flicker down to his phone before he spoke. "I gotta head out. I only came in to pick up lunch. Where are you stayin'?"

I tried to hide my disappointment at the mention of him leaving. "Sophia offered me the apartment above The Ridge until I find a place, but it won't be ready for a couple of days. Is there a motel nearby?" I replied.

"No way in hell I'm lettin' you stay at that grimy motel on the other side of town," Jake shot back firmly.

I was caught off guard by how straightforward he was, and my confusion was evident on my face. "Why not? I don't have a lot of options here, Jake. I'm short on cash and a motel is the cheapest option."

Jake gripped the edge of the table like he was trying to keep his cool. "It's not a safe place, Sarah. The guy who owns it is shady as fuck. A lot of sketchy people hangin' around. You're not stayin' there."

I should be pissed he is trying to tell me what to do, but I'm not.

Instead, his genuine worry warms me. It's the complete opposite of how Michael used to control me and make every decision for me. Jake's requests come from a place of care and worry, while Michael's demands were always about dominance and control. It had been so long since anyone but Anna cared about me. "Thank you for looking out for me, but I have to take what I can get. Like I said, I don't have a lot of money to get by until I start working."

"Darlin', it's OK, I got somewhere for you to stay and it won't cost you anything." He flashes me a smug grin and then adds, "and I won't have to worry about you being alone at that motel. It's like you'd be doin' me a big favor by staying there. You do want to help your BFF out, don't you?"

Not able to hold back my grin, "you're terrible, you know that right? Thanks for being terrible Jake, it's really nice."

Sophia suddenly appeared with a brown paper bag in her hand, interrupting our conversation. "I brought your lunch order, Jake. I didn't want it to get cold sitting at the bar." Jake nods, "thanks Soph. I'm going to take Sarah down to the B&B and get her settled in a room."

Turning to me, Sophia gestures for me to stand. As I do, she wraps me in a tight hug, "go get some rest. Come by tomorrow morning and I'll start training you on the breakfast shift. It's slower paced, so it's a good one to start with." Then she whispers in my ear, "He's a good guy."

"Sophia, I am incredibly grateful for this job and all that you are doing for me. Please know that. I'll be here in the morning. It was lovely to meet you."

"No worries, hun. You go get some rest, and we'll catch up tomorrow. And don't forget to let me know about that apartment upstairs." Sophia turned and headed back to tend the bar.

"Come on Darlin', let me walk you over to the B&B and show you where you'll be staying." Jake said as he gestured for me to follow him out of The Ridge. Once we were outside, he reached over to take my backpack from where it rested on my shoulder.

My body instinctively recoiled, a conditioned response from years of abuse. "I'm sorry, I just wasn't expecting that." I felt embarrassed by my reaction, but Jake didn't say anything, just took my bag and slung it over his own shoulder in one smooth motion.

I followed Jake's confident strides down the street, back in the direction of the bus station where I had arrived. He slowed his strides to match my much shorter ones, a comforting gesture that made me feel at ease. We walked side by side, he briefly rested his hand at the small of my back, gently guiding me along the bustling sidewalk. The small town hummed with energy, and I couldn't help but feel grateful for Jake's presence next to me as we made our way through the busy streets.

As Jake walked with me down the sidewalk, he started making conversation. "So... I'm guessing you moved out here on your own. No man in the picture?"

I didn't want to tell Jake the situation I was in. "The simple answer is no, there isn't a man in my life. But the more complicated answer deserves its own discussion. How about you?"

Nodding, Jake replied, "Alright then, no men for either of us, glad we're on the same page. No woman either. There was this one a while back, total knockout, great ass. One day she just up and ghosted me. Left me with some serious trust issues." He turned and flashed his signature teasing smile, giving me a playful wink. I realized he was talking about me.

"See? You really are terrible!" I teased back, playfully bumping into him with my shoulder. Jake burst into deep laughter, the sun glinting off his bright eyes.

"Oh come on, babe. I'm not that bad," he chuckled.

Looking ahead, I nodded in agreement, "No Jake, you're really not bad at all."

CHAPTER 6

Sarah

The final stretch of our walk was filled with a heavy silence, but the tension between us spoke volumes. Being near him again awakened feelings I thought were gone forever. A sense of possibility, however fragile, fluttered tentatively to life in my chest.

Lost in my thoughts, we arrived at a grand Victorian house without me even realizing it. The home was nestled among towering pines that framed the sides of the property. A carefully manicured front yard greeted us with a rainbow of tulips lining the walkway to the porch. Hanging wicker baskets filled with lush green ferns adorned the white posts of the porch railing, and window boxes bursting with colorful blooms and cascading vines added to the charm of the home.

Jake led me up the old porch steps, and just as we reached the front door, it opened without us having to knock. Standing inside was an elderly woman with silver curls and the same gray eyes as Jake's. As soon as she saw him, recognition spread across her face.

"Jake, what a surprise! Come on in, both of you." Jake gave my hand a reassuring squeeze as we stepped inside. Up close, I saw she had the same strong nose and chin as Jake.

Jake introduced me to his grandmother, Marlene, with such warmth and love in his voice that it made me smile. Marlene then wrapped me in a gentle hug, her floral perfume and soft sweater creating an aura of comfort around me.

I caught a glimpse over Marlene's shoulder of the cozy antique furnishings and floral wallpaper that adorned the interior of the house. It emanated a sense of warmth and love, truly feeling like a home. Marlene slowly released me.

"Gram, would it be alright if Sarah stays in my old room upstairs for a bit?"

"Of course, she can." Marlene answered with a hint of annoyance in her voice. As if it was completely absurd Jake would even ask.

"It would be nice to have some company. I'd be delighted if you'd stay here, dear." Her kind, brown eyes scanned my face intently. "You can stay in Jake's old room for however long you need."

I tried to hold back the tears threatening to spill, moved by her unexpected kindness towards someone she didn't even know. Jake placed a comforting hand on my shoulder. "You need anything, you let me know. My place is at the far end of the property, right behind here. Just go out the back door and follow the gravel driveway through the trees."

Jake embraced his grandma tenderly. "I really appreciate this, Gram. I have to head back to the garage." Then turning to me, "Sarah, I'll swing by later to check on you once I'm done for the day."

"Jake, dear, will you stay for dinner tonight?"

He turned towards his grandmother, "I wouldn't miss it, Gram." With a final nod in my direction, Jake made his way out through the front door.

Marlene showed me upstairs to a cozy suite tucked under the eaves. A four-poster bed was draped in quilts, lending a cozy feel. Lace curtains fluttered gently over the windows, and a worn armchair sat in one corner beckoning me to sink into its embrace.

"The bathroom is just across the hall dear, towels are under the sink." Marlene gave my arm a tender pat. "You get some rest now. We'll talk more this evening. I'll have dinner ready at about 6:00, I hope you'll join us."

Alone in the quaint bedroom, I sat gingerly on the edge of the quilt-covered bed and looked around. Sunlight streamed through the window, bathing everything in a warm glow. The space was comforting with a homey feel, everything the home I shared with Michael wasn't. For the first time in longer than I could remember, I felt completely at peace.

I walked over to look out the window. The pine trees were dark silhouettes against the bright blue sky, their needles rustling in the gentle breeze. The tin roof of Jake's trailer glinted in the sunlight, peeking out from behind the trees at the edge of the woods.

I sink into the plush bed, and a wave of relief washes over me. I had finally escaped from Michael's grasp. Now, with Jake by my side, I could potentially have a friend here, I won't be completely alone. It was like I could finally breathe again, after being suffocated for so long.

The gentle tapping on my bedroom door slowly woke me up. "Sarah, you up?" Jake's deep voice carried through the wood, and I groggily responded with a muffled yes. I stumbled to the door, half-awake. When I opened it slightly, the cool air of the hallway hit my bare legs and I realized I wasn't fully dressed. Jake's gaze trailed down my body, taking in my disheveled appearance before quickly snapping back up to my face.

"If you're hungry, Gram made dinner. She would like it if you would eat with us at the table," Jake said, leaning against the door frame and a relaxed smile on his face. "I wouldn't mind it either."

"I'd like that, I'll be down in a minute." With a shy smile on my face, I closed the door behind me.

I could hear the murmur of conversation between Jake and his grandma in the kitchen as I descended the stairs. They stopped talking when they saw me enter.

"Come on in, dear, and have a seat. Are you hungry?" Marlene asked, already preparing a plate of food for me. "I'm glad you got some rest."

"I just wanted to say thank you again, to both of you."

Marlene waved a dismissive hand at me. "It is no trouble at all, dear. Any friend of Jake's is always welcome. Although, you are the first female he has ever brought home. I was beginning to think he had a preference for male company."

I blushed and shifted my gaze to the ground while Jake cleared his throat awkwardly. "Gram, no more whiskey before dinner."

The easy affection and playfulness between him and Marlene warmed me. She was the grandmother I'd always dreamed of having.

As we sat down to dinner and enjoyed some delicious roasted chicken and veggies, I found myself sharing fond memories from my past with Jake. Marlene was an attentive listener, asking for more details about Jake's teenage years. His playful protests only made me laugh even more.

After dinner, Jake walked me out to see the stars from the back porch. I settled on the wooden swing with a contented sigh. Jake leaned against the railing, hands in his pockets as he studied the night sky. The full moon cast everything in a dreamy glow.

"Jake..." My voice came out barely above a whisper. His eyes snapped to mine, soft and questioning. "Thank you for this. For being here. It means a lot to me."

Jake was quiet for a moment before coming over to sit beside me in the swing. He took my hands in his larger, rougher ones. The contact zinged through me like electricity.

"I meant what I said about being here if you need anything Sarah." His gray eyes locked earnestly with mine. "No matter what happened before, I'm just glad you ended up here."

Tears sprang unbidden to my eyes at his heartfelt words. Without thinking, I leaned over and pressed a soft kiss to his stubbled cheek. Jake's breath seemed to catch at the contact.

After a paralyzed moment, he squeezed my hands and stood. "I better call it a night. But I'll see you tomorrow, okay?" He waited for my nod before descending the porch steps, walking towards the gravel driveway leading to his house..

I watched him walk away, my lips still tingling from the kiss. The swing continued to sway gently as I sat marveling over how a place I just arrived in could feel more like home than anywhere I've ever been.

CHAPTER 7

Jake

As I trudge down the lengthy driveway towards my house, I can hear the gravel crunching beneath my boots. I turn my head to look back and see Sarah still sitting on the porch swing on the back porch.

It has been fourteen years since I saw her, and yet she still has me by the balls in a way no other woman has. Even at 18 years old, I never thought I would find someone more attractive than I did Sarah. If my younger self could see her now, at 30 years old? Yeah, I would have been trippin' over my own god damn tongue. Her chestnut hair cascades in gentle waves down her shoulders, just as it did when we were kids. Her eyes still shine a brilliant green, but there is a hint of sorrow behind them that wasn't there before.

I force myself to turn back around and keep walking to my trailer. My mind is reeling, trying to process the total mindfuck that was today. When I walked into The Ridge earlier, I thought I was seeing a ghost. I just froze like an idiot, unable to form a coherent thought as I stared at her in disbelief.

When I first saw her, my initial reaction was to be tough on her. After all, she had left me fourteen years ago and I was still holding onto years of resentment and pain. But then Sarah began to tell me the whole story - about the letters that never reached me and how she was sent to another foster home. Her voice trembled as she spoke, tears threatening to spill from her eyes. And in that moment, I knew she was telling the truth. My girl hadn't abandoned me after all.

I ran a hand over my stubbled jaw and let out a heavy sigh, wishing I had reacted better. Sarah deserved my patience and understanding right off the bat, not my short-tempered accusations. We were just stupid kids back then, barely old enough to understand the shit hand life had dealt us both. I should've known Sarah would never give me the brush off without reason. She needed someone in her corner just as much as I did back then.

I didn't even realize I'd made it all the way down the tree-lined driveway to my small single-wide trailer. Home sweet home. I step inside the familiar space, tossing my keys onto the counter. The fridge hums softly in the corner as I grab a cold bottle of beer and collapse onto the worn leather couch.

I take a long sip from the bottle and relax back against the cushions, closing my eyes. Everything had seemed so normal this morning. My usual routine - up at dawn, quick breakfast, then off to open the shop. Around lunchtime I headed over to the Ridge to pick up a sandwich. And that's when my world got flipped on its ass.

Memories from the day keep playing in my mind like short film clips. I can see Sarah's smile as we shared jokes while walking to the B&B. The slight tremble in her voice when she asked if I lived in North Ridge now. And the gratefulness in her shy demeanor when I offered for her to stay at Gram's place.

Her flinch as I reached for her backpack wasn't a normal reaction to a sudden movement, despite how she tried to downplay it. I could recognize that it was a trained reflex, honed from being in dangerous situations. I know this feeling well; when you're constantly surrounded by potential threats, your body and mind adjust to the environment. You become hyper aware of any dangers lurking around you. She's clearly running from something or someone, and her instincts are still on high alert.

I take another swig of beer, lost in my own head. Can't stop thinking about how Sarah leaned in to press a kiss to my cheek before I left the porch tonight. Such an innocent gesture, but it rocked me to my core. I feel like such a pussy. I need to get a fucking grip, I'm not 18 anymore.

My eyes snap open when I hear the roar of an engine approaching the house, bright lights cutting through the darkness and illuminating the living room. I'd recognize the sound of Rex's Harley anywhere. Sure enough, seconds later he's pounding on my front door.

"It's open," I call out.

Rex steps inside, his tall muscular frame barely fitting through the doorway.

"Hey brother, we need to talk." I raise an eyebrow at his serious tone.

"What's going on?"

He reaches into the refrigerator and pulls out a cold beer, then plops down onto the recliner next to the couch. "I should be asking you that question. Where the hell did you disappear to during your lunch break today? You were gone for over two hours, and we needed you back at the shop. You're the only one that can do the fabrication work on the Henderson bike. It's not going to be done tomorrow. We almost sent out a damn search party."

"Sorry man, I just got caught up."

"Caught up, huh? This have anything to do with that hot little number I saw you walking with earlier?" I wanted to wipe that smug ass smirk right off his face.

Irritated, I hesitate. Reluctant to get into everything with Sarah so soon. "Ran into someone I hadn't seen for a long time and lost track of time catching up. I'll call Henderson tomorrow and explain that we are going to be a day behind."

Rex's eyes narrow, like he can sense I'm holding something back. "This someone have a name?" When I don't immediately answer, understanding passes over his face. "It was her, wasn't it? Sarah, that girl you used to know as a teenager. The one who vanished."

I sigh, nodding slowly. No point trying to hide anything from Rex. He's my cousin, but he's also my best friend. I give him a condensed version of running into Sarah and getting her set up at Gram's place.

Rex lets out a low whistle when I finish. "Damn, brother. That's one hell of a blast from the past. You told me stories about this girl over the years, and it sounded like you really loved her, even if you were both young. How are you handling seeing her again after all this time?"

I rake a hand through my tousled hair, buying time to think. "I don't know man. It's a lot to process. On one hand, I'm thrilled to see her again. Never thought I'd get that chance. It's a relief knowing she is OK, the never knowing what happened fucking killed me. But part of me is still pissed, you know? I spent so long thinking she wanted nothing to do with me. Now here she is again."

Rex nods, "I get that cuz, makes sense you're all mixed up about it. But it seems like she had a good reason for leaving, and she came back to see you again when she could. You had just already left for basic. Maybe this is your second chance, brother. To get back what you lost. If she meant something to you, and you think she could again, don't hold yourself back with all the shit running around in that head of yours. Trust me if I had a chance to get back what I lost, I'd be all over that. Sure as shit wouldn't be sitting in this trailer with your sorry ass right now."

I stay silent, staring down at the bottle clutched in my hands. Rex has a point. As confusing as it is to have Sarah back in my world again, it also feels like I've been given a gift.

I feel like total shit when it finally dawns on me what Rex meant by, "if I had a chance to get back what I lost." It's been four years since his wife, Rebecca, was killed in a car accident right after I moved to North Ridge. Fortunately, their daughter Emmalynn was unharmed; the car seat she was in saved her life. She was only two months old at the time.

Rex finishes his beer and stands, clapping me on the shoulder.

"Whatever happens next, I've got your back brother. But do yourself a favor and don't let the past ruin what's right in front of you now. I gotta get home. I'm sure your sister is ready to leave, she's been taking care of Emmalynn all day. We have a meeting tomorrow before you go to the shop. Dad's got a new skip to track down."

After I got out of the Marines, I found myself working alongside Rex and my uncle Beau at the club's bail bonds business, 'Riggs Bonds & Bounty'. With my background, bounty hunting came naturally to me.

After walking Rex outside, I grab another beer from the fridge and return to my spot on the couch. My thoughts drift back to Sarah. The time spent with her on Gram's porch tonight. Her tiny hand fitting perfectly inside my rough, weathered one. The gentle touch of her lips against my cheek.

I couldn't even think straight enough to come up with a decent excuse to stay longer. Just mumbled some lame ass excuse about needing to call it a night and damn near jogged off that porch. Not my smoothest move. I didn't want to risk spooking her after the way she reacted to me reaching for her bag earlier.

My protective instincts for Sarah snapped back into action as soon as I laid eyes on her. I won't let her stay in that shitty motel.

She's either staying with me, or at Gram's B&B. And she can forget about moving into that apartment above The Ridge. Sarah didn't know it yet, but I planned on being around as much as possible to drive her to and from work. Just thinking about her making that trip, walking alone in the dark made my stomach twist. North Ridge may be a safe community, but danger still lurks. I'm not going to let anything happen to her, not while I'm here to protect her.

I yawn and rub my eyes before getting up to toss my empty bottle in the trash. It's getting late and I have an early start tomorrow. Before I hit the sack, I make sure to set an alarm for 5 a.m. on my phone. That'll give me enough time to grab us some coffee and breakfast, then swing by and pick up Sarah before she starts her first shift at The Ridge.

◆ ◆ ◆

The buzz of my 5am alarm jolts me awake. I fumble to silence it and sit up slowly, scrubbing a hand over my face. It's still dark out, but I need to get moving if I'm going to pick Sarah up and make it to The Ridge by 6:30 am when her shift starts.

I hop in the shower to wake myself up, letting the hot spray soak my shoulders and back. The water pounds against tired muscles, rinsing away the last remnants of sleep. After toweling off, I get dressed and add an extra layer for warmth against the morning chill. The weather is starting to get a little warmer now during the day, but the mornings are still cold in April. Before leaving, I make sure to grab my keys and wallet.

Rushing, I quickly make my way to the only cafe open at this ungodly hour on Main Street. I ordered two large coffees and three breakfast sandwiches to-go. By the time I make it back to

Gram's place, the first signs of dawn are slowly appearing on the horizon.

I drive down the private road that Gram uses to access the back of her house, which is separate from the public parking for the B&B. As I make my way up the porch stairs, I carefully balance a tray of coffee and a bag of takeout in my hands. From inside the house, I can hear the sound of dishes being set on the breakfast table in the kitchen. I knock gently on the door before entering, causing the heavy oak door to creak loudly. Gram greets me with a warm smile, her soft gray curls falling around her face.

"You're up bright and early, Jake," she remarks, giving me a knowing look. We both know the only reason I'd be awake before dawn.

I raise the coffee carrier and takeout bag. "I brought breakfast. Sarah up yet? I planned on giving her a ride to The Ridge for her shift." I put the bag down on the table and dig through it for the ham and cheese croissant that I know is Gram's favorite.

"So sweet of you, dear." Gram beams at me and gives my cheek a gentle pat before calling out to the stairs. "Sarah? Jake is here to give you a ride to work."

A moment passes before I hear light, quick footsteps on the stairs. My heart starts racing as I see Sarah coming down, looking far too awake for this early hour. Her hair is loosely braided over one shoulder, and she gives me a shy smile.

I really need to get my shit together.

"Jake, I hope you didn't think I expected you to give me a ride. You're already doing so much for me; you don't have to drive me to work too. I appreciate it but I don't want to take advantage of you."

"OK, a few things we need to address real quick. First, I do have to drive you to work. It's cold, it's dark, and you don't have a car. No way in hell I'm about to let you walk alone when it's barely light out. Second, feel free to take advantage of me anytime you'd like, really, I insist. Hope you like your coffee," I add with a wink as I hand her the cup.

Sarah's cheeks flush with embarrassment. "You're a lifesaver, and still a little terrible," she teases as she takes the coffee from me. "I can't believe you just said that in front of your grandma."

"Darlin' I think Gram knew I was down for you to take advantage of me when I showed up on her doorstep at six in the mornin' with coffee and breakfast in hand. This is not a typical mornin' for me."

"Sure did." Gram adds her two cents from behind us before taking a bite of her croissant.

After saying our goodbyes to Gram, we make our way out to my truck. I open the door for Sarah and she gives me an amused smirk. "I didn't realize you could be a gentleman." Grinning, I quickly jog around the front of the truck to get in. I turn up the heat so that she'll be warm during the drive.

We make small talk during the brief car ride, discussing how she slept and if there is anything else she needs while staying at the B&B. I can't help but notice how close Sarah is sitting beside me in the passenger seat, her flowery fragrance blending with the rich smell of coffee that fills the cab of my truck.

As we sit at a red light, I steal a quick look at her. The warm light of the rising sun catches on her hair, making it shine. She senses my gaze and turns to meet my eyes. Suddenly, there's a shift in the air between us, like an electric current passing through the space.

The light turns green, snapping me out of my thoughts. I clear my throat and refocus on the road. I tighten my grip on the wheel, mentally kicking my own ass. *Get it together, man. She's been back less than 24 hours. Here you are, acting like a dumbass schoolboy with a crush.*

Just as my thoughts start to spiral, The Ridge appears in front of me. I quickly turn into the back parking lot and find a spot to park. "I picked up a breakfast sandwich for you, not sure what you're into these days. I just ordered your old favorite."

I hand her the sandwich and take mine out of the bag. She averts her gaze, but I catch a tear rolling down her cheek. Gently, I brush away some loose strands of hair from her face and tuck them behind her ear. "Darlin', did I do something to upset you? If you don't like this sandwich, I can get you something else. I just wanted to make sure you didn't go hungry all day."

"You didn't upset me, Jake. I'm sorry, I feel so stupid. I can't believe you remember what breakfast sandwich was my favorite after all this time. This is perfect, thank you. I'm starving actually." Embarrassed, she tries to gather her belongings to get out of the truck.

"I don't think so, babe." I reach across the bench seat in my truck and wrap my arm around Sarah's waist, effortlessly pulling her onto my lap.

"Jake, stop, you're going to hurt yourself. I'm too big for this." She turns her head away, not wanting to meet my gaze. I place my hands gently on either side of her face, turning it towards me so she has no choice but to look at me.

"I need you to listen to me, Sarah. No matter what the reason, you don't ever have to apologize to me for havin' feelings. If your upset, I want to know so I can fix it. Your feelings are not stupid, or insignificant to me. As far as you thinkin' you're too big to be in my lap, that's bullshit Sarah. Look at how well you fit here, up against my chest. You're fucking perfect. Now, hand me your phone so I can add my number. I'll be waiting here at 3:30, right when your shift is over. If you get out earlier, just text me."

"I don't have a phone. I left mine back in Oregon."

Yeah, she's definitely fucking running from someone.

I tenderly stroke the side of Sarah's hip where my hand rests. "Alright Darlin', go on inside so you're not late for your first day. I'll be back at 3:30."

"Thanks again for the ride, Jake." Sarah jumps out of the truck and swings her purse over her shoulder. She flashes a smile and waves before disappearing inside. I take a moment to gather myself before heading over to Riggs Bail & Bounty. My thoughts keep returning to Sarah, like a moth drawn to a flame without any control over its direction.

CHAPTER 8

Jake

The familiar neon sign buzzes overhead as I pull into the parking lot of Riggs Bail & Bounty, our clubs bail bond and bounty hunting business. I cut the engine and head inside to meet with my uncle Beau and Rex, unsure what this early morning skip meeting is about.

Riggs Bail & Bounty is just one of the businesses the club owns around town. We also own the garage I manage, Son's Customs, and The Ridge. My grandfather was a founder of the Rebel Sons MC, the first President, and one of the original six members. After he stepped down as Pres, my uncle Beau took the seat at the head of our table as President and Rex as VP.

The door chimes announcing my arrival. Beau looks up from his desk and waves me into his office. Rex is already sprawled casually across one of the leather chairs, boots propped up on the edge of Beau's mahogany desk.

"Mornin' sunshine," Rex teases as I drop into the seat beside him. "Nice of you to finally join us."

I shoot him the finger discreetly where Beau can't see. "Shut it, Rex. I'm here, ain't I?"

Beau clears his throat pointedly and Rex drops his feet to the floor. His expression turns serious as he slides a file across the desk towards us.

"Got a new skip for you boys. Client is Bowen Bail Bonds a few towns over. They bonded out this guy arrested in a prostitution sting who decided not to show for his court date."

I flip open the file skimming the details. No record, no registered firearms. Quiet life working some corporate IT job until he got busted. Your average middle-aged suburban john, not anyone expecting to be brought in on a bench warrant. An easy grab and go.

"I know the sheriff over in Whitefish," Beau continues. "I'll give him a courtesy call letting him know we'll be operating in his county. Then I'll get Wyatt and Jax to track down the skip's current location."

He leans back in his leather chair, folding his hands over his chest. "Soon as we verify his whereabouts, I want you two to head over and bring him in. Shouldn't take more than a day. I told Bowen we'd have this guy wrapped in forty-eight hours."

I nod, flipping the file closed and passing it back across the desk. Rex and I both stand to take our leave. Before I can make it out the door, Beau calls out to me.

"Hold up a sec, Jake. Got something else to discuss with you."

I linger in the doorway as Rex claps me on the back.

"Catch ya later, bro. I'll be at the shop when you're done playing kiss ass." He ducks the swat I aim at his head and laughs on his way out.

Shutting the office door, I turn back to Beau with a questioning look. "What's going on?"

He leans forward, clasping his hands on the desk. "I wanted to check in, see where your head is at. How you're handling our unexpected visitor in town."

Rex has the biggest fucking mouth.

I scrub a hand across my stubbled jaw, buying time. Trust Beau to cut right to it. "I'm alright," I hedge. "It was a shock running into her, but I'm workin' through it."

Beau studies me with those knowing eyes that seem to see straight through bullshit. "Mmhmm...so that's why you've been trailing around after her like a lost puppy?"

I glance away, feeling exposed. Was it that obvious how rattled I was by Sarah's reappearance?

"Look son," Beau continues, his gruff voice gentling. "I know you cared deeply for that girl once upon a time. I also know life's handed you a tough road." He pauses, brow furrowing. "Just don't want to see you get hurt if things go sideways again. Or let the past cost you your future."

I scuff my boot across the worn office floor, considering his words. "I appreciate the concern, but I gotta see where this goes, you know? She's...she's something special."

Beau nods slowly, seeming to accept this. "Alright then. I'm here if you need an ear. Or bail money. Now get on outta here, daylight's wasting."

A smile creeps onto my face as I head towards the parking lot where my truck is parked. I need to get over to the shop and get some work done before we start our skip hunt. But my thoughts are already focused on picking Sarah up after her shift ends.

I swing by the general store to grab a prepaid phone for Sarah. Then, I make my way to the shop, ready to lose myself in work for a few hours.

I pull up to the corrugated metal building that houses Sons Customs, my eyes immediately spot Rex's sleek black Harley parked out front, right beside my own. The sound of muffled rock music drifts out from the open garage door as I make my way inside. The air was thick with the scent of motor oil and gasoline, and I could see Rex, his arms buried deep under the hood of a classic Chevelle.

I quickly change into my worn overalls, and join him in the cluttered garage. I get right to work finishing up a custom motorcycle for one of our clients.

Around noon, Rex wanders over, wiping his greasy hands on a rag. "I'm starving, man. Wanna head over to the Ridge for some grub?"

I hesitate, not sure I want Rex hounding Sarah for details. "I got some paperwork to finish up on the Henderson bike."

Rex claps me on the back. "Come on, brother. The paperwork can wait another hour. I'm buying."

Sighing, I give in and follow him out to the parking lot. I'll just have to do some redirecting if he starts prying into things with Sarah. I don't want him making her uncomfortable.

We ride over to the tavern, parking our bikes out front. Inside, Rex grabs a table near the bar while I go order us a couple beers at the counter. Out of the corner of my eye, I see Sarah clearing dishes from the far end of the bar, laughing at something Sophia said.

God she's beautiful when she smiles like that. Grabbing the chilled bottles, I make my way back to Rex and take a long pull, hoping the cold beer will shock some sense into me. A moment later, Sarah approaches our table, order pad in hand.

"Hey Jake."

"Hey Darlin', this here is my cousin Rex. Rex, this is Sarah."

Her smile is soft and genuine as she glances my way before turning to Rex. "It's nice to meet you Rex. What can I get you guys?"

"I'll take a bacon cheeseburger with fries, sweetheart" Rex drawls with an easy grin.

"I'll take the same thing." Sarah dutifully scribbles down our order, tucking her pen behind her ear.

I watch warily as Rex leans back in his chair, clearly appraising her. "Jake didn't mention he knew such a pretty little thing around here." Before I can jump in, he continues smoothly, "You been in town long? Don't think I've seen you in here before."

Sarah's eyes flicker towards me, a silent question. It's as if she's seeking my permission to speak to him. Her actions make me feel uneasy. I give her a nod. *Why does she feel she needs my permission to speak to someone?*

"I just got into town yesterday actually. Today is my first day."

I give her a smile when Rex glances down to take a sip of his beer.

Soon our food arrives courtesy of Sophia. As we eat, Rex keeps up an easy flow of small talk, telling Sarah about life in North Ridge and the shop. I add comments here and there, but mostly just observe their interaction.

Despite his imposing size, Rex has always had a certain charm with women. Probably because he actually respects them, unlike most of the assholes around town just looking to get laid. Still doesn't stop an irrational flare of jealousy when he makes Sarah genuinely laugh out loud.

Finishing up our beers, we get ready to head out. As Sarah clears our plates from the table, I hear her and Sophia discussing her living situation. The apartment upstairs will be ready by the weekend Sophia mentions. Before I can think better of it, I find myself cutting in.

"That's real kind of you Soph, but it won't be necessary. Sarah's got a place to stay." I ignore Sarah's glare in my direction, keeping my eyes on Sophia.

After a beat, Sophia just smiles. "No problem at all, honey. You let me know if you change your mind."

Sarah gave me a forced smile and a polite goodbye, but her eyes betrayed her true feelings, anger and disappointment. The subtle twitch of her lips suggested that she wanted to say something, but instead she just continued on back behind the bar. That was a dick move, and I knew it.

Walking out of The Ridge, Rex elbows me with a knowing grin. "My, my, ain't you just full of surprises. And laying down the law." He shakes with laughter at my irritation. "Ah lighten up, I'm just playin' with ya."

Back at the shop, I lose myself in engine repairs and custom paint jobs for the next few hours, trying to avoid glancing at the clock every five minutes.

Finally at 3:20, I leave Rex at the shop. I climb on my bike and head over to the Ridge to pick Sarah up. The late afternoon sun casts a warm glow as I pull into the small back lot, cutting the engine. I run a hand through my hair and smooth my shirt before heading inside in search of Sarah.

I find her behind the bar, laughing with Sophia as she wipes down the gleaming wooden surface. Our eyes meet across the room and her face brightens. *Maybe I didn't piss her off as much as I thought.* She says a few parting words to Sophia before making her way over, untying her apron as she walks.

"Hey," she greets me with a shy smile. "Thanks again for the ride this morning. And for coming to get me."

"Anytime, Darlin'. How was the rest of your shift?" She tells me about her day as we exit the tavern and walk to the back lot where I parked. Sarah's expression turns curious when she sees me remove a small box from my saddlebag before turning to her.

"Got you somethin'." I press the prepaid phone into her hand, watching emotions play across her delicate features. "Figured this would make things easier until you get a new phone. Already programmed my number in there for you."

Sarah turns the phone over in her hands, seemingly at a loss for words.

"You didn't have to do this Jake, really. It's too much."

I brush my thumb gently across her cheek. "It's just a phone, Sarah. I want to make sure you can reach me if you need me." Unable to resist, I add with a teasing grin, "Definitely need to make sure you can reach me if you change your mind about taking advantage of me, anytime, day or night."

Sarah's cheeks turn a pretty shade of pink as she playfully hits my shoulder. "Such a troublemaker." Despite her words, a smile tugs at the corners of her lips as she carefully puts her phone away in her pocket.

I grab the helmet hanging from my bike's handlebars and carefully place it on Sarah's head, ensuring that the strap is securely fastened under her chin. I then stow her purse in my saddlebag before mounting my bike. I offer a hand to help Sarah climb onto the seat behind me, and she wraps her arms around my waist as soon as she's settled. *Good Girl*

Exiting the parking lot behind The Ridge, I make a turn towards the B&B. As I come to a stop at a red light, I reach over and place my hand on Sarah's outer thigh, giving it a gentle squeeze, lightly stroking my thumb up and down.

I raise my voice over the noise of my bike, "You good, Darlin'?"

She leans in closer, her body pressed firmly to my back, her mouth right behind my ear. "I'm good."

The drive to Gram's house seemed to pass by too quickly. The feeling of her body against mine was something I didn't realize

I had missed so damn much. As soon as Rex and I wrap up this bounty hunt, I'm going to take Sarah out for a long ride.

Pulling up the gravel drive, I cut the engine and help Sarah off my bike. "I gotta head back to the shop," I explain. "I have a few loose ends to tie up and some more hours to put in before leaving for a bounty job tomorrow. I'm gonna leave my truck here. You can drive it to work while I'm gone."

Even as I spoke, she was already shaking her head. "Sarah, please just do this one thing for me. I don't want to spend all day at work tomorrow worrying about you walking alone to and from your job."

"Alright, Jake. Thank you."

I reach into my saddlebag and grab Sarah's purse and phone box, handing them to her. "I'll text you when I get back into town tomorrow," I tell her with a kiss on the forehead. I resist the urge to do more, and pull away quickly, even though there is so much more on my mind.

CHAPTER 9

Sarah

The chime of the door opening greets me as I step into The Ridge Tavern. Sophia's face lights up when she sees me.

"Sarah! So glad you're here, honey. You ready for your first day?" Her enthusiasm is contagious, and I can't help but smile back.

"I think so. A little nervous, but mostly just excited to get started."

Sophia gives my shoulder a reassuring squeeze.

"You're gonna do just fine. We'll start off easy with training on the breakfast shift. Then work you up to taking full tables at lunch and dinner as you get the hang of things."

I nod, appreciating her thoughtful approach. Sophia proceeds to give me a full tour of the bar area and kitchen, showing me where everything is located. She grabs a server's apron and ties it around my waist.

"Alright, let's dive in. I'll walk you through using the POS system to enter orders and take payments. Then we'll go over serving drinks, running food, bussing tables - the works!"

Over the next few hours, Sophia patiently guides me through the different tasks, letting me shadow her as she handles customers. Watching her flawlessly juggle multiple tables, I feel both amazed and daunted. But Sophia just smiles encouragingly.

"Don't worry if you don't pick it all up instantly. Took me months to get in the groove when I first started here. You'll get the hang of it."

Right around 9:00, the breakfast rush began. My nerves spike but I take a deep breath and grab a pot of coffee, preparing to take my first table. I channel Sophia's grace under pressure as I go through the motions she taught me - greeting the customers, taking orders, delivering food and drinks. To my relief, everything goes smoothly.

The morning rushes by as I balance plates and serve customers, gradually becoming more at ease in the busy atmosphere. Every so often, Sophia stops by to give me helpful pointers where I could improve.

Around noon, I hear the door chime and look up from my task of restocking menus. My heart races as I see Jake and another man entering the tavern. My eyes are drawn to Jake in his faded denim jeans and leather kutte. When he notices me looking, his lips give a slight twitch, hinting at a smile, before he heads towards a table near the bar.

Grabbing my order pad and pen, I take a steadying breath. I can do this. Just another table. Smoothing my apron, I paste on a polite smile and approach their table.

"Hey Jake." I turn my smile briefly to the other man, who Jake introduces as his cousin, Rex. "What can I get you guys?"

Rex drawls an easy request for a bacon cheeseburger and fries. When I look to Jake, there's an intensity in those stormy eyes that makes my cheeks grow warm.

"I'll take the same, Darlin'." His rough voice on that term of endearment sends a little thrill through me.

I quickly jot down their lunch order and head back to the kitchen, releasing a sigh of relief. Those two must think I'm a total idiot, getting so flustered just by taking their order. But every time I see Jake, it throws me off balance. I really need to get a grip.

I deliver their beers, then check on my other tables while their food is cooking. A while later, I spot Sophia heading into the hallway that leads to her office. Impulsively, I caught her arm.

"Hey Soph, about that apartment..."

Before I can get the question out, Jake's voice cuts in from behind me.

"That's real kind of you Soph, but it won't be necessary. Sarah's got a place to stay."

I whip my head around to glare at him. Who does he think he is, answering for me? Sophia just smiles kindly.

"No problem at all, honey. You let me know if you change your mind." With an understanding pat on my hand, she heads to her office.

I resist the urge to speak out, not wanting to draw attention from the other customers. I can't help but feel frustrated and let down on the inside. As I clean up after Jake and Rex's meal, I try to push through my shift, counting down the minutes.

Wiping down the gleaming bar one final time, I untie my apron just as Jake enters. I force my expression neutral and bid Sophia farewell before making my way over. No point in more confrontation, not until we can talk privately.

"Thanks again for the ride this morning. And for coming to get me." My attempt at being polite comes out awkwardly, even to myself. I can't bring myself to look directly at him for too long, still overwhelmed by the emotions his gaze stirs in me.

Jake's tone holds a note of uncertainty. "Anytime, darlin."

Outside, he secures the spare helmet on my head then stows my purse away. I press myself tightly against his strong, muscled back, finding comfort in his presence. Looks like I'll be holding off on that talk until later.

As we come to the first stoplight, I'm surprised when Jake's hand reaches back to gently stroke my thigh. My heart races at the unexpected touch. The tender caress of his thumb manages to ease some of the stress from the day. For a brief moment, I let myself fully enjoy his touch, appreciating the affection behind it.

By the time we reach the B&B, my earlier upset has diminished to a dull ache. Jake explains he has to return to the shop to finish up some work before leaving town tomorrow. I don't press for more details, knowing it's not my place to ask.

Once inside, Marlene greets me and I find myself enveloped in one of warm hugs. I cling to this woman who somehow always knows exactly what I need.

"Come help me get supper on, Dear. You can tell me all about your day." I follow Marlene into the cozy kitchen, the knot in my chest already loosening. I fill her in on the day's events as we prepare chicken parmesan. She clicks her tongue sympathetically when I describe Jake overriding my apartment decision.

"Men often have a misguided notion that they know what's best for us womenfolk. Suppose it's on account of caring a bit too much." She gives me a wry smile. "Not excusing poor Jake's behavior, mind you. He needs reminding you have your own say."

I nod, considering her words. Maybe Jake was just trying to help in his own clumsy way. Still didn't give him the right to make choices for me.

After we tidy up the kitchen, Gram digs out a tin of chocolate chips from the pantry along with a smudged recipe card. "How about we make my famous chocolate chip cookies? It's a secret recipe, but I want to teach you. Maybe it will brighten up your mood." She playfully nudges me and manages to coax a small smile from me.

As we mixed the butter and sugar together, our conversation flowed easily. We added eggs, flour, and chocolate chips to the mixture. I took this opportunity to ask Marlene about her life, genuinely curious and eager to learn more about this amazing woman.

A hint of longing fills her gaze as she recounts memories of her late husband, Jacob. She tells me how they fell in love at a young age and built a beautiful life together. Then how she supported him in his decision of starting the club and then built the Rebel Sons into what it is today. I admire the quiet strength in her as she describes losing him a few years back, just before Jake returned from his final tour overseas.

My curiosity gets the better of me, and I gently ask about Jake's childhood before I knew him as a teenager. Marlene measures her words, obviously cautious.

"Jake's mother left home at 18 and cut off all communication. We would have to search for her every time we wanted to reach out. She struggled with addiction after meeting Cassandra and Wyatt's father, but she never revealed who Jake's father was. Her overdose when Jake was only 15 left him responsible for raising his younger siblings until he joined the military. I had only seen Jake a few times before he enlisted, but he made sure to send Cassandra and Wyatt to me before he left. It was clear that their father was not fit to be around any of the children.

I lay a comforting hand on her arm, encouraging her to continue. She pats my hand, eyes growing damp.

"Jake's never had it easy, but he made something of himself. I'm so proud of the man he's become." The depth of love in her voice makes my own eyes water.

As I crawl under the covers in my room that night, I feel a deep sense of belonging. Like this is the home I never had growing up, being shuffled between uncaring foster families. Marlene's unconditional love and support means everything.

The next morning, I woke up to a sweet text from Jake.

> *Jake: Good morning, beautiful. I'm in Whitefish with Rex, picking up this skip. If everything goes smoothly, I might be back in time to get you from work. I left the keys to my truck on the kitchen counter. It was late when I left the shop, I didn't want to wake you.*

> *Me: Be safe out there. Glad to hear you boys have everything under control. Don't get yourself into too much trouble ;)*

> *Jake: Who me? Never ;) I'm always a perfect angel. I'll have you know I'm a mature, level-headed professional. Rex keeps me in line.*

> *Jake: We okay?*

I pause, considering. As much as Jake's behavior bothered me, I know it came from a place of caring.

Sarah: We're okay. Looking forward to you being back in town. Stay safe.

Jake: Always ;) I'll check in with you later. Miss that pretty smile of yours already.

I slide my phone into my purse and get ready for work before heading downstairs. Marlene greets me with a cheery smile and plate of flapjacks.

We chatted over breakfast about my schedule for the day. I help tidy up the kitchen, before heading out to Jake's truck.

I arrive at The Ridge just as Sophia is flipping the 'Closed' sign to 'Open.' Her eyes light up when she sees me. "There's my girl! Ready to tackle day two?"

Her enthusiasm is contagious. I grin back. "Absolutely. What do you need me to do first?"

Morning prep work goes swiftly with the two of us working in easy harmony. By the time early customers start filing in, I feel fully prepped. Sophia and I trade off waiting tables and manning the counter, the hours slipping by unnoticed.

Around 3:00 the bar phone rings. Sophia answers, then turns to me holding out the receiver. "It's for you, honey. It's Anna."

My pulse kicks up, immediately concerned that something is wrong. Taking the phone, I manage a steady "Hello?"

Anna's voice is barely audible as she speaks quickly. "Sarah, thank God. I only have a minute before Michael gets back. He's still suspicious, he doesn't trust me. He even hired someone to investigate."

A wave of fear hits me, causing my knees to buckle. I grab the counter edge for support. We were so careful covering my tracks. What proof could he possibly find that I'm alive?

Anna's tone becomes urgent, "You need to be careful. Michael won't stop until he finds answers. Promise me you'll stay safe. I'll —" Her frantic words cut off abruptly.

The line goes silent except for the dull tone signaling an ended call. My hands shake as I return the receiver to its cradle. I lean heavily on the counter, head spinning. Just when I thought we were in the clear, the nightmare returns. If Michael discovers I'm here...

I struggle to make it through the remainder of my shift, feeling like I'm in a daze as my thoughts spin nonstop. After work, I head straight back to my room at the B&B, purposely avoiding Marlene. Collapsing onto my bed, I reach into my pocket and retrieve my phone. There is a text waiting for me from Jake.

> *Jake: Hey Darlin', sorry I didn't make it back in time to grab you after your shift. This skip decided to make a run for it. Total shit show. But we got him in custody now and I'm headed home soon.*

> *Sarah: No worries, glad everything ended up OK. Are*

you free tomorrow? I was hoping we could talk.

Jake: I'm all yours sweetheart. I know we got some things to talk about.

Sarah: Do you have the day off?

Jake: Yeah, shop's closed on Sundays. You got the breakfast shift at the Ridge?

Sarah: I'm off too.

Jake: Good. Wanna go for a ride with me tomorrow? There is a spot about an hour from North Ridge I'd really like to show you. We can take a lunch and talk there.

Sarah: That sounds really nice. I can put together some sandwiches and snacks.

Jake: Sounds perfect darlin'. I'll pick you up around 10 tomorrow morning?

Sarah: Can't wait :) See you then. Drive safe tonight!

Jake: Always do. Goodnight sweetheart.

CHAPTER 10

Jake

I pull up to the back of the B&B on my motorcycle Sunday morning, looking forward to spending the day with Sarah. The fresh morning air is crisp and the sky is clear. I send Sarah a quick text to let her know I'm here, before sliding my phone back into my jacket pocket.

A few moments later, the back door slowly opens and Sarah steps outside. She's wearing well-fitted jeans that mold to her curves in all the right places, and that same hoodie she had on the day she arrived in town. On her arm, she carries a small basket, which she raises in greeting as soon as she spots me. My pulse kicks up a notch at the sight of her smiling face. I can't help but smile back, drinking in how beautiful she looks with her long brown hair blowing softly in the breeze. Damn, she looks good enough to eat. I dismount and climb the creaky porch steps to meet her, taking the basket from her hands.

"Mornin', beautiful," I say, unable to resist brushing a lock of silky hair behind her ear.

Sarah's cheeks flush prettily. "Morning, Jake."

Leading Sarah to my bike, I set the basket down to help Sarah with her helmet. Her green eyes find mine as she looks up at me through long lashes. It takes all my self-control not to pull her body into mine and kiss her soft, full lips. Instead, I gently press my lips against her cheek, breathing in her sweet floral scent.

"All set darlin'?"

With her confirming nod, I secure the basket and then throw a leg over my bike. I offer my hand to help Sarah climb onto the back, and she settles in behind me, wrapping her arms around my waist. I give her hands a reassuring pat before starting the engine.

"Hold on tight, sweetheart."

The engine roars to life beneath us as I pull out onto the open road. We cruise through the countryside, past rolling green hills and open fields. The spring breeze feels amazing whipping around us. Every so often, I glance back to see Sarah's hair blowing wildly behind her, a huge smile lighting up her face. She seems so happy and carefree. I like seeing her like this.

An hour passes as we continue to ride, until finally I make a turn onto a winding dirt road that leads deep into the forest. Eventually, the road opens up to expose a hidden gem - a sparkling blue lake surrounded by towering mountains in perfect seclusion.

I cut the engine and set down the kickstand. "Here we are. Welcome to my favorite spot."

"Jake, this is gorgeous! How did you find this place?"

I grin, pleased by her reaction. Not many outsiders know about this place. "I found this place not too long after I moved to North Ridge, out on a ride. Been comin' here ever since when I need to clear my head. Thought you'd like it too."

I help Sarah off the bike then grab a folded blanket and the basket. We choose a flat spot on the lakeshore, shaded by tall pine trees, and spread out the blanket. The soft sound of the water lapping at the shoreline combines with birdsong and rustling leaves overhead. Sarah closes her eyes, tilting her face up to soak in the peaceful setting.

"It's so beautiful here," she says softly.

"Yeah it is." I'm looking right at her, not the surroundings. Sarah meets my gaze and her cheeks flush that pretty pink again.

Sarah has really outdone herself with the lunch she prepared for us. There are thick roast beef sandwiches, pasta salad, fresh fruit, a platter of assorted cheeses, and even homemade chocolate chip cookies for dessert. I grab a couple of cold beers from the small cooler as we make ourselves comfortable on the blanket, sitting across from each other.

I notice Sarah avoids the beer, choosing a bottle of water instead. I make a mental note but don't press the issue, not wanting to pry if she's avoiding alcohol for personal reasons.

We dig into the food, between bites, Sarah asks about my work as a bounty hunter, seeming genuinely interested in what I do. I give her the rundown on how we track down the skips who miss their court dates, carefully leaving out some of the seedier details. She asks me about some of the crazier skip chases and I tell her exaggerated tales of danger that make her laugh.

After we've finished eating, I pack up the remainder of the food while Sarah spreads out on the blanket. We decided to walk along the edge of the lake to explore more of the area. The conversation flows easily between us just like old times, I'm still surprised by how comfortable and natural things feel with her.

We eventually circle back to our spot and sit facing the water, shoulders touching. My hand finds hers, interlacing our fingers. "I'm so glad you came out here with me today."

She gives my hand a soft squeeze but stays quiet, lower lip caught between her teeth. I can tell there is something troubling her. I know I should address the issue of the apartment above the bar.

"About the other day at Sophia's... I'm sorry for interfering the way I did. I should've talked to you first before sticking my nose in your business."

Sarah gives me a grateful look. "Thank you. I just... I've spent so many years having no control over my life. My choices were never my own. Even small things. So when you answered for me, it triggered some bad memories for me."

Sarah gives me a soft smile but it soon fades. She stays quiet, clearly struggling with something. I wait patiently, sensing she's working up the nerve to open up more.

After a few moments, she takes a deep breath and turns to face me fully. "Jake, there's a lot I haven't told you yet. About where I've been and how I ended up in North Ridge. I want to tell you everything but it's not easy for me. I hope it doesn't change how you see me."

I squeeze her hand supportively. "You can tell me anything, Sarah. Nothing could make me think less of you."

She nods, glancing down for a moment to gather herself before meeting my gaze again.

"After I finished high school, I waitressed at a diner downtown. After work one day, I met Michael."

Her lips twist bitterly around his name. I remain silent, just rubbing my thumb over her hand in what I hope is a comforting gesture.

"He seemed so charming at first. Handsome, confident, smart. He offered me help when I didn't have anyone else. I was young, desperate, naïve, and way too trusting. Before I knew it, we were married."

She pauses, staring off at the water again. I sense the worst is yet to come. My chest tightens but I keep quiet, letting her take this at her own pace.

"As soon as we were married, he started changing. Little comments putting me down about my weight or how I was dressed. He would get furious if I spoke to any other males or didn't follow his every command.

The first time he hit me was about a month into the marriage. I was in shock, couldn't believe someone who claimed to love me could hurt me like that. I forgot to record his sports game on TV. He backhanded me so hard I fell to the ground. And then came the apologies, always the apologies. He would blame stress or alcohol or find some way to pin the blame on me. I was so young and stupid, desperate for stability and a sense of home, I tried to forgive him every time. But deep down, I knew that was not how love was supposed to feel."

Red hot rage courses through me at the thought of anyone laying hands on Sarah. But I resist the urge to interrupt, letting her get this out.

"His words were so convincing that I truly believed it was my fault. The apologies and gifts he gave me after made me think he really didn't mean to hurt me, I just push him too far. But it always happened again, and over time, it only got worse. The apologies eventually stopped, but not his fists. I have endured broken bones and the scars..." She turns her arm to show a jagged mark running along her forearm.

I ghost a finger over it, jaw clenched.

"There's more than that one." Her voice cracks on the last words. She's staring down at the blanket now, shoulders hunched. I move closer and wrap my arms around her. After a moment she relaxes into me, I feel some of the tension leaving her body.

"He controlled every aspect of my life. Wouldn't allow me to work or see friends. Cut me off from anyone who could've helped me. And at night..."

Sarah's voice falters as she speaks, but the meaning in her words couldn't be clearer. My vision blacks out at the edges as the full scope of what she endured sinks in, and rage like I've never felt before tries to take over. Years of brutal violence, confinement, and sexual assault. And I didn't have a damn clue.

"As time went on, the abuse became a daily occurrence. He would strike me, kick me, and throw things at me. Each time, he made sure to aim for places where the bruises could be hidden by clothing. One day, he broke my wrist and lied to the ER about how I got injured, claiming I had fallen down the stairs.

The physical abuse was awful but the emotional abuse was even worse," Sarah says so quietly I have to strain to hear. "The names, the constant criticism, blaming me for everything, controlling everything I did or who I talked to. After so many years of it, you start to believe what they say about you is true. That you're worthless, nothing without them."

Her voice breaks on a sob. I just hold her tighter. How could anyone treat this incredible, beautiful woman with anything less than complete devotion?

"Shhhh, I've got you now, baby. You're safe with me" I whisper into her ear. "I'm right here, I'll never let anything like that happen to you again."

We stay in that position for a while as Sarah's sobs gradually turn into quiet sniffles, releasing the pain she's bottled up for years. I gently rub her back, providing comfort until her tears eventually come to a stop. She sits up, wiping her eyes and sniffling. I caress her cheek, brushing away the remaining trails of tears with my thumb.

"That fucker had you convinced because it gave him power. But it was all lies, Sarah. You are amazing and strong. Don't ever believe otherwise."

Sarah takes a shaky breath, steeling herself before continuing.

"The sexual abuse... at first he was almost gentle, and I tried to convince myself it wasn't so bad. Then it became more violent, he was more aggressive. He..." Her voice falters for a moment. "He forced me to do things that made me hate myself, made me feel so disgusting and dirty."

Despite the boiling rage within me, I push it down and remind myself to stay calm for Sarah's sake. She needs me to be present and focused, not consumed by thoughts of revenge. I gently take her hands in mine and crouch down to meet her gaze.

"You have nothing to feel ashamed of, Sarah. The fault lies with him alone. However you survived, you did what you had to in that situation. Don't let him continue hurting you with misplaced guilt."

Sarah searches my face, relief washing over her features as what I said sinks in.

"A few weeks ago, I found out I was pregnant." One hand unconsciously moves to rest on her stomach. "I knew I had to get us out."

I suck in a sharp breath as her words sink in. Pregnant. Sarah is pregnant, a child conceived in violence but one she clearly already loves. No wonder she left. I'm sick to my stomach thinking about everything she's had to endure.

Sarah avoids my gaze, obviously worried about how I will respond. With a soft touch, I lift her chin until our eyes meet.

"You being pregnant is what you were worried about tellin' me? Thinkin' I would look at you differently if I knew?"

Tears continue to stream down Sarah's face as she nods her head slowly. I use my thumbs to gently wipe them away, while cradling her face in my hands.

I smooth back her hair, letting all the love and tenderness I feel for her show on my face.

"It changes nothing Sarah. That baby your carryin' is a part of you, and there isn't a damn thing about you that I don't love. You wanna give this thing between us a go, I'm all in. You just wanna be friends and keep things the way they are, I'm here for you. Either way, you're not alone anymore if you don't want to be. I'm gonna be here for you, and that baby, however you both need me."

Sarah's cheeks are stained with fresh tears, and before I can even process what's happening, she throws her arms around me, burying her face in my neck as she holds onto me tightly.

"Jake, there's something else I need you to know. When I left, I wrote a suicide note and faked my death. Anna, Michael's sister, helped me. She called me at work yesterday and told me Michael didn't buy it and hired a private investigator. In the middle of the call the line went dead. I think he caught her calling me. He's coming for me, and he will find me."

"Don't worry about it baby, I'll take care of it. I'm not gonna let anyone or anything touch you. You'll always be safe with me."

We stay locked in each other's arms as the sun dips lower behind the mountains, the world narrowing down to just us. Two damaged souls finding solace and understanding. No more words need to be spoken. After what feels like hours, I help Sarah to her feet and gather up our things. The ride back to town is quiet, Sarah's arms wrapped snugly around my waist.

The weight of everything she revealed to me today is still heavy on my mind. The fact that she suffered through years of abuse only reignites my anger. But even more powerful is my determination to protect Sarah and her child. I'll die before I'll let any harm come to them again.

The motorcycle rolls to a stop in the driveway of the B&B as the sun sets behind us, casting a dusky glow over the sky. I turn off the engine and prop up the kickstand, helping Sarah get off the bike. I lead her up to the back porch, and she hesitates before going inside, gazing up at me with uncertainty.

Taking her delicate hands in mine, I meet her conflicted gaze.

"I meant what I said about bein' here for you, Sarah. Let me stay with you tonight so you don't have to be alone. We can stay here if you're more comfortable, or head over to my place."

Sarah considers this for a moment, then gives a small nod. Relief floods through me knowing I'll be able to keep her close and provide some sense of safety. She deserves so much more than this, to always feel safe and cared for unconditionally.

We head inside and up the back staircase quietly, not wanting to disturb Gram this late. Once in Sarah's room I wrap my arms around her curvy frame from behind and she melts back into me with a content sigh. We stand holding each other in the quiet darkness of her room, drawing comfort just from our closeness.

Eventually we get ready for bed. I strip down to my t-shirt and boxers while Sarah changes into an oversized sleep shirt in the bathroom. She crawls under the covers with me.

"Will you hold me?" she asks in a small voice.

"Of course, baby." I pull her to me, her back nestling against my chest. She relaxes into my embrace, her body fitting so perfectly with mine. I breathe in the sweet scent of her hair and smooth one hand over the barely discernible swell of her belly. A fierce wave of protectiveness sweeps over me for the precious lives curled up safely in my arms.

I continue lightly stroking Sarah's hair long after she falls asleep, staying awake late into the night planning our next steps. First thing tomorrow, I'll call Rex and Beau, bring them up to speed to get their help trying to get a location, and some background information on Sarah's ex. If that bastard shows his face anywhere near my girl again, I'll fucking kill him. I'll go to hell and back to make sure they are safe.

CHAPTER 11

Jake

I wake just as the first rays of dawn begin to filter through the window, casting a soft glow over Sarah's sleeping form curled against me. She looks beautiful with her hair fanned out across the pillow, lips slightly parted as she breathes deeply. I brush a feather-light kiss to her temple before carefully pulling my arm from under her head. She murmurs something unintelligible and snuggles deeper into the blankets but doesn't wake. I find a scrap of paper and scribble out a quick note.

Sarah,

Had to head to the shop for a bit this morning. I'll be back later, baby. You rest up.

-Jake

I tuck the paper under her phone on the nightstand where she's sure to see it, then grab my jacket and boots. With one last lingering glance at Sarah, I slip quietly out the door and head downstairs.

The B&B is still silent as I make my exit out the back door, the morning air crisp and damp with dew. I'll need to hustle to get the shop opened on time.

The rumble of my bike shatters the early morning quiet as I pull away down the road leading back to town, dawn just beginning to break over the silhouette of the mountains.

My thoughts are consumed with processing everything Sarah revealed, the horrific details she entrusted me with yesterday. I've gotta talk to Rex and Beau, get 'em up to speed on just how dire this situation is. I need to track down that sadistic bastard and make damn sure he never lays a hand on her again.

I pull up outside Rigg's Bail and Bounty just as Rex is unlocking the front door, coffee and a bag of donuts in hand.

"Mornin'. Brought breakfast," he says, holding up the goods. His smile fades as he takes in my grim expression. "You good, man?"

"We gotta talk. Now. Where's Beau?"

I brush past him, walking straight into Beau's office, stripping off my jacket and getting right to the point. "It's about Sarah. I was with her yesterday and she told me some things. Awful fuckin' things about what she's been through with her Ex."

Just saying those words causes my blood to boil all over again. Rex's eyebrows shoot up but he remains silent, waiting for me to continue.

"She's on the run. She moved here hoping no one would find her here. The bastard she's running from, her husband... he's a violent son of a bitch. Nearly beat her to death more than once. Broke bones, scars all over her body. Kept her trapped, no money, nowhere to go. Nobody to help."

Beau's face hardens as the severity of it sinks in. His jaw clenches and I can see his mind turning over what I'm telling him.

"She said he forced himself on her. Often. Fucker should be skinned alive for what he did to her."

I spit the words from between gritted teeth. If I ever lay eyes on the fucker, they'll be hauling me off to prison cause I'll kill him with my bare hands for what he did to her.

"Christ. Poor girl's been through hell." Beau shakes his head, a storm brewing behind his eyes.

"There's more." I run a hand roughly through my hair. "She's pregnant. The baby...its his. But she's determined to protect it, give it the life she never had growin' up."

Rex, scrubbing a hand down his face, "Explains why she hightailed it outta there. No way would that coward let his punchin' bag and his kid just up and leave."

"Exactly. And if he ever finds her, I got no doubt he'd kill her and not think twice." My voice sounds rough and anguished just vocalizing that possibility. Not gonna happen. Not on my watch.

Beau breaks the heavy silence. "Alright Son, what do you want us to do?"

"Rex, I need you diggin' into this guy however you can. Full background check, aliases, known addresses, criminal record, financials. Anything to give us a lead on where he is, and a heads up on where he might be headin'."

Rex nods, lips set in a grim line as he drops into his desk chair and wakes up the computer. "I'll run the checks through every database we got access to. Even call in a favor or two if I need to." His fingers are already flying over the keys as he starts hunting for intel.

Beau turned his attention to me, "You wanna call in the rest of the club on this, Jake? You know Jax could dig up a lot more than what we can."

"No, not yet. Right now it's a family matter, and I'd like to keep it that way out of respect for Sarah. I'm sure she doesn't want everyone knowing about her past. If she does that's her story to tell. If we would need back up for anything, we can take it to the table and it will be up to Sarah what information I share about what happened to her."

"Alright Son, that sounds like a plan. While Rex gets to work on the computer side of things, I'm gonna cash in a favor with Diaz over in County, see if he can run this bastard's name through the system, maybe dig up any active investigations or warrants. I'll call in a few other markers, quietly put some feelers out. See what shakes loose." Beau states while already picking up the phone to make the call.

"I appreciate whatever you can turn up, Beau."

"No problem. That poor girl's been through more than anyone should have to. We'll make sure he never hurts her again, or the kid."

Beau's parting words echo my own thoughts. I won't rest until Sarah and her baby are safe.

◆ ◆ ◆

The next few hours pass in a blur of paperwork, phone calls, and new bike designs, as I try to keep myself occupied at the garage. But thoughts of Sarah are never far from my mind.

Around noon, my cell lights up with Rex's number flashing across the screen.

"What'd you find out?" I answer, forgoing any greeting.

"You ain't gonna like this, brother. Michael Moretti, Sarah's husband. He's a Fed, and not just any Fed. Guy is DEA, a Special Agent working out of the Portland field office. The fucker comes with a stack of commendations. He's gotten results for them so they turn a blind eye to his methods from what I gather. He's suspected in a handful of excessive force complaints that mysteriously disappeared. And this is just what I could dig up on the surface. He seems to have some heavy hitters covering for him. I know you didn't want to take this to the club, but we might have to. If this fucker comes looking for her, then finds out she's with you. There could be some serious blowback on the club. The last thing we need is DEA sniffing around."

"Son of a bitch." I scrub a hand over my face. This is worse than I could've imagined. If he finds Sarah here, no telling how far he'll go to get her back under his control.

"Rex, I need you to keep digging. Get everything you can on where he operates, any properties owned, anything. Call in favors if you need to."

"You got it. I'll shake the trees, see what else falls out. Meantime, you keep our girl and that baby safe, ya hear? She's been through enough hell."

"I plan to. Thanks Rex."

I end the call feeling even more on edge than before.

Around mid-afternoon, I finally wrap up at the garage and head over to the B&B hoping Sarah is still there. The place seems quiet when I pull up. I let myself inside, moving quietly up the backstairs to Sarah's room. I give a soft knock and when there's no answer, I carefully crack the door open.

"Sarah?" I call out gently.

The room is empty, bed neatly made. No sign of her. My heart kicks into overdrive, panic rising in my chest as I quickly scan the room just to be certain she isn't here. Dammit, where is she?

I force myself to take a deep breath, trying to think rationally. Maybe she had a morning shift at the Ridge. I'm halfway to my bike, ready to speed over there to check when my cell vibrates in my pocket. I fumble getting it out, nearly dropping the damn thing in my haste.

It's a text from Sarah.

> *Sarah: I didn't want to bother you, so I caught a ride into work with Marlene. I figured you had a lot on your plate after everything I unloaded on you yesterday. I'll understand if you need some space to process it all. No pressure. I don't want you to feel obligated or overwhelmed though. I get it if it's too much with the pregnancy news and all. Just know I appreciate you being there for me. It meant more than you'll ever know. Stay safe*

Damn. My leaving this morning without talking to her first probably reinforced those fears. If she's worrying I'm having second thoughts, I need to erase those doubts real quick.

My bike roars to life and I steer it toward town, anxious to have Sarah back within eyesight. I find a spot right out front of the Ridge and park my bike. I stride through the doors, eyes immediately searching for Sarah. I spot her behind the bar, refilling ketchup bottles. Her face brightens when she sees me, lips curving into that sweet smile that makes my chest ache.

I see Sophia coming out of the kitchen, "Soph, can Sarah take a break for a few minutes?"

"Sure, we just cleared out the lunch rush. Go ahead and take a break Sarah."

I walk with purpose around the bar and take Sarah's hand, leading her down the hallway that goes to Sophia's office and the stockroom. I pull Sarah into the stock room and close the door behind us.

"I'm sorry about takin' off this mornin' without talking to you first. Didn't mean to worry you, just had some things to take care of." I smooth back her hair, looking intently into her eyes so she grasps my meaning.

"I should've woken you. I don't want you thinking for one second I have any doubts, not after you bared your soul to me yesterday." My voice comes out gruff with emotion.

Unable to resist, I brush my lips over hers. Just a fleeting kiss but enough to convey the simmering need that's been growing between us. When I pull back, her cheeks are flushed that pretty shade of pink I love.

I brush my lips over hers again, this time lingering for a moment, tasting her sweetness. My free hand slides down her back, pulling her closer to me as our bodies press against each other. I trace small circles on her lower back before sliding around to cup her belly gently.

"I just want you to know... I'm not leavin' you to face this alone, alright? I'm in it for the long haul, if you want me to be." The kiss deepens as our tongues dance slowly, teasingly against each other's lips. Our need for one another is palpable; it's like an ache inside us both that can only be soothed by the other. Our breaths quicken, skin flushing under the fluorescent lights of the stock room. Lost in the moment, forgetting everything but each other.

My hands slip under her shirt, tracing the delicate skin of her lower back. "I missed you this morning," I admit quietly. She moves closer, her arms wrapping around my neck. I savor the warmth of her body against mine as she buries her face into my neck, inhaling deeply.

"Missed you too," she whispers before meeting my lips once more. Our kisses grow more urgent now.

My mouth finds her neck. My lips and tongue trace a path along her soft skin, stopping just below her ear. I can feel her pulse quicken against my lips, her body reacting to my touch.

"We shouldn't be doing this here," she whispers against my skin.

"I know." Damn, this woman is like a drug to me.

My hands glide with ease around the curves of her hips, moving to cup her round ass. I pull her tightly against me, feeling every inch of her warmth and softness pressed against me. A low, sensual moan escapes her throat, sending shivers down my spine and straight to my dick. I can't resist grinding my hips against hers, the friction and intensity only fueling my desire for her even more.

"Goddamn it," I growl out against her lips, just before pulling away. "We gotta get out of here." Taking a deep breath, I try to regain some control. Looking into her eyes, I can see the desire still burning there. "Better not keep Soph waiting, babe," I whisper against her lips before pushing open the door and stepping out into the small hallway.

I grab Sarah's hand, slowing her down. "Hey babe? I meant to ask you earlier... There's a spring festival in town this weekend to raise money for charity. Food, games, music. Was hoping you'd come with me. I'll be working the grill at the Rebel Sons booth for a bit, but I'd like for you to be there. Meet some more of my family, my brothers."

Sarah smiles, green eyes sparkling. "I'd love to. That sounds really nice."

I brush my lips over her hair. "Yeah? How about I cook us up some steaks tonight at my place, and you spend the night with me?"

"That sounds really nice too."

"OK darlin', I'm going to run over to the butcher shop, pick us out a couple of steaks. I'll be back to pick you up from work. You go get back to work before you get me into trouble with Soph."

CHAPTER 12

Sarah

As I finish cleaning the bar, I sneak a look at the clock once again. My shift is almost over, and I'm counting down the minutes until I can leave. As soon as Sophia gives me permission to go, I toss my apron under the counter and grab my purse before heading out through the back door of the Ridge.

Jake's battered blue truck is parked right outside the door when I step outside, classic rock filtering softly out the open window. He must have been waiting out here for a bit, but he doesn't seem bothered, just happy to see me. As I walk up to the passenger door, he reaches across and pops it open for me.

"Couldn't wait to get outta there, huh?" Jake grins as I slide onto the worn leather seat beside him.

"You have no idea," I sigh, letting my head fall back against the headrest, eyes slipping closed. The faded cab smells of motor oil, leather, and that familiar scent of Jake that makes me feel warm and safe inside.

Jake's rough fingertips push aside a strand of hair that had escaped my ponytail, then glide gently along the curve of my jaw. I turn my head to face him, and as I open my eyes, I am met with his gentle gaze and a small smile playing on his lips.

"Long day?" His voice is gentle.

I sigh heavily. "So long, my feet are killing me." I lean towards him, enjoying the feeling of his fingers gently kneading my neck. A small sound of contentment escapes from my mouth without me even realizing it.

Jake chuckles, "Why don't you put your feet up on the dash, I'll give you a foot rub when we get back to my place."

I respond with a playful tone, "Watch out, I might actually take you up on that offer." The idea of Jake's skilled hands massaging the tension from my aching arches is already appealing.

When he laughs, the faint lines at the corners of his eyes show, and his stormy grey irises seem to light up with a special warmth reserved only for me.

As we drive to his trailer, tucked behind the B&B, our conversation flows effortlessly. The tension that once existed between us has dissipated, and now it feels natural to chat about our days. I recount an incident with a rude customer who snapped their fingers at me like I was a dog for not refilling their coffee fast enough. Jake's jaw tightens as he shakes his head in disapproval. I can't help but imagine how differently the situation would have gone if Jake had been there; the customer would have received more than a few choice words about treating people with respect. It's comforting to know that I have someone on my side now.

I'm still adjusting to our changed relationship. This newfound intimacy between us. I can't pinpoint the exact moment when Jake became my protector, my sanctuary. The person I can rely on and confide in without hesitation. It happened so organically that I almost didn't register the transformation. But now, I can't imagine not having him by my side. Thank goodness he walked into The Ridge that day, and back into my life like an unexpected savior I didn't realize I was missing.

Jake turns, steering the truck off the main road and onto a gravel lane that winds past the B&B, through a thick grove of towering pine trees. When we pull up to the trailer, he quickly hops out and walks to my side. Opening the door for me and extending his hand to help me step down from the high seat.

The crisp evening air is a pleasant change from the tavern. I take off my flannel shirt, leaving me in a black tank top, and enjoy the sensation of the breeze on my exposed arms. Jake's eyes track my movements, but he keeps a respectful distance. When I catch him looking, I give him a reassuring smile. We're still trying to navigate our relationship, treading carefully around each other's boundaries. Sometimes it feels like there's an electric charge between us, pulling us together. But Jake never forces anything, letting things develop at a pace that makes me comfortable.

I spot Jake already starting the grill off to the side of the trailer and can't help but smile.

"I hope you're hungry. I picked up a couple nice Sirloins from the butcher shop earlier."

At the mention of steak, my stomach gives an audible rumble and I press a hand over it self-consciously. Jake just grins.

"I'll take that as a yes. Potatoes are just about finished baking inside too. I tossed them in the oven before I picked you up." He nudges open the trailer door, the smells of roasted garlic and potatoes wafting out into the dusk.

"It smells amazing in here. You really didn't have to go through all this trouble just for me."

Jake just shakes his head like I'm crazy for even suggesting such a thing, holding the screen door for me to step inside.

"It's no problem, really. It gave me something to look forward to."

His genuine words bring tears to my eyes, and I quickly turn my head to look out the small kitchen window at the dark pine forest. No one has ever done something so kind for me without expecting something in return. With Michael, there was always a price, some strings attached. But Jake is different; he gives from the goodness of his heart without asking for anything in return.

Jake expertly flips the steaks on the grill, a faint sizzle filling the air. I chop up fresh vegetables and toss them into a bowl, drizzling dressing on top. As we work together, a sense of warmth and familiarity settles over us. It's as if this is a nightly ritual for us, even though it's only our second date. The coziness of domestic life wraps around us like a warm blanket.

During dinner, I ask about Jake's day at the garage and the bike he's currently designing. I could listen to him talk about motors and horsepower all night long, the passion clear in his voice.

As the conversation slows down, I gather my courage and mention the appointment I made earlier. "I wanted to let you know... I have my first prenatal appointment on Monday morning at the Mason's Women's Health Clinic. I know it's a bit of a drive, and short notice if you had something else planned..."

I let my words taper off, and I lower my eyes to poke at a roasted potato on my plate. A sudden wave of anxiety washes over me as I worry that I may have assumed too much by thinking he would want to be there. We haven't really discussed the details of him joining me for appointments or what it all means for our future. He has already done so much for me, and maybe it's not fair for me to depend on him like this. I don't want him to feel trapped or obligated in any way.

"Sarah."

I feel his fingers under my chin, gently nudging me to meet his eyes again. His expression is serious but soft when he speaks again.

"You know I want to be there with you, right? For anything you need. Appointments, tests, everything. However much or little you want me there, I'm gonna be by your side unless you tell me otherwise." His thumb ghosts over my bottom lip and I close my eyes, leaning into his touch.

"You sure you don't mind? I know that's a lot to deal with when it's not even…" I trail off mid-sentence, a lump forming in my throat. Not even his child. The unspoken words linger heavily between us for a moment.

Jake slides his palm along my jaw, turning my face more fully towards his.

"Remember what I told you the other night. I'm in this for the long haul, darlin'. You and this little one ain't in this alone anymore." He gently places his strong hand over my stomach. Despite the fact this isn't his biological child, the gesture of protection and love brings tears to my eyes. I rest my hand over his, our fingers threading together.

"How did I get so lucky to have someone like you?" I whisper, feeling grateful beyond words.

"I'm the lucky one, sweetheart."

The endearment slides off his tongue so naturally it makes my heart flutter like a lovesick schoolgirl. I have to resist the urge to lean across the table and kiss him senseless.

We finally stand up to tackle the dinner dishes, Jake washing while I dry and put away. I take note of where everything belongs in the cabinets. It's comforting being here with him, doing everyday tasks together. We are slowly becoming a part of each other's lives, one small step at a time.

As we finish cleaning up the kitchen, I cover my mouth with my hand to hide a yawn. It has been a long day.

Jake gives my shoulder a gentle squeeze. "Why don't you take a quick shower while I finish up here? You mentioned your muscles were sore earlier, and it might help you relax."

A hot shower does sound amazing right now. I smile gratefully and head towards the small bathroom. I push open the bathroom door, flipping on the light switch. Like the rest of Jake's place, the bathroom is simple but has everything I need. I turn the knob in the shower, letting the water heat up as I slip out of my work clothes. Stepping under the hot spray feels heavenly, the perfect pressure pounding against my knotted muscles.

I take my time, standing under the hot water as it cascades over me, rinsing away the dirt and sweat from a busy day. I inhale deeply, savoring the earthy, masculine scent of the soap. It's the same smell that lingers on Jake's skin and clothes, providing a sense of familiarity and security. Just the faint reminder of him is enough to make me feel content and at ease.

My mind wanders as I linger under the spray, thinking about how things have been since inviting Jake fully into my world and my pain. Giving voice to all the horrors I endured lifted a tremendous weight from my shoulders. I feel lighter now, hopeful even. Like freeing those demons opened up room for good things to finally grow.

Despite learning the ugliest, most shameful parts of me, he hasn't pushed me away. If anything, sharing my past brought us closer together. I've never trusted someone so completely before. Never felt this safe or cherished.

Is it crazy that just a week ago he was nothing more to me than a fond childhood memory, and now I'm halfway to picturing a life with this man?

My skin is flushed and pruned by the time I finally shut off the water. I wrap myself up in one of Jake's big plush towels. It's worn soft from use and smells like him. I take my time patting myself dry before wiping the fog from the small mirror above the sink.

I stare into my reflection critically for a moment. The dark circles under my eyes do little for my appearance, but at least my cheeks have more color to them now. But the scar on my collarbone serves as an ever-present reminder of why I'm here.

Shaking off those memories, I dress quickly in my panties and camisole. I finger comb through my wet tangles before braiding my damp hair loosely over one shoulder. It's still early evening but I'm looking forward to cuddling up in bed, maybe watching a movie together.

Rummaging under the sink, I find an extra toothbrush Jake must keep for guests. After brushing my teeth, I catch a glimpse of one of Jake's t-shirts slung over the towel bar. Without overthinking it, I slip the worn cotton shirt over my head. It falls to mid thigh on me, the soft fabric enveloping me in Jake's warmth and the smoky, masculine scent I now associate solely with him. I lift the fabric to my nose and breathe him in, letting the familiarity wrap around me like a blanket.

The shower shuts off in the other bathroom just as I step out into the hall. I must have lost track of time in my own indulgent shower. Padding down to the cozy living room, I curl up on the corner of the couch. I hear Jake moving around in the other room for a few minutes before the door opens.

"Sorry I took.." I glance up and the sight of him makes my words freeze mid-sentence, mouth suddenly parched. Rivulets of water still cling to his hair and the planes of muscle on his bare chest. The sweatpants hung low on his hips do nothing to conceal his sculpted abs or the tempting vee of muscle that disappears beneath the waistband.

A single bead of water slowly trails down over his chest, following the grooves of his torso before disappearing into the cotton clinging to his hips. I can't tear my eyes away from the entrancing movement.

Jake's lips twitch with amusement at my obvious attention, but he doesn't gloat. He simply takes the towel from around his neck and gives his damp hair another rub. My brain needs to form words but all coherent thought has apparently fled in the wake of six feet of hard muscled, gorgeous man on display.

"Sorry, hope you don't mind. Gets too damn hot for a shirt after a shower." Jake's deep voice snaps me out of my trance, and I quickly redirect my gaze back to his face, feeling my cheeks heat up in embarrassment for being caught staring so openly.

"No! I mean - yes, that's totally fine. You should be comfortable." I stutter out awkwardly. *Smooth Sarah. Real smooth.*

If Jake notices how flustered I am, he doesn't call attention to it. He simply drapes the towel over a chair before making his way to the fridge.

"You want a beer or somethin'?" He asks over his shoulder.

"I uh...I better not. With the pregnancy." Words are still not coming easily with him distracting me by rooting around the fridge bare chested.

"Shit, sorry. Wasn't thinking." He grabs a bottle of water instead and joins me on the couch, sitting close but not touching.

I tuck my legs up under me and lean into the soft leather, acutely aware of his body heat along my side. We're both shower fresh and relaxed. It would be so easy to curl into his warmth and lose myself for a while. But I don't want to make any assumptions about where his head is tonight.

Jake takes a long swig of his drink before turning more fully to face me.

"So I meant to ask...how have you been doin', staying at the B&B?"

"Being at the B&B has been better than staying at a motel, that's for sure. Marlene is so sweet to me, I really enjoy spending time with her."

Jake reaches over and takes my hand loosely in his. "Are you happy over there?"

I nod, playing with his fingers, focusing on them rather than meeting his eyes. "I am. She really feels like family. But I can't rely on her generosity forever."

Jake tilts my chin up with a finger so I have to look at him.

"You know you're welcome here anytime, Sarah. I meant it when I said I want to be here for you."

A lump forms in my throat at how sincerely he means that. I just nod, unable to speak around it. Seeming to sense I'm getting emotional, Jake squeezes my hand.

"You want to watch something?" He grabs the remote off the coffee table.

"That sounds perfect." I tuck myself into his side as he searches for something to watch, his solid warmth a comfort.

We settle on an action movie that looks entertaining but not too deep, or heavy. As the opening chase scene unfolds on screen, I feel Jake absently playing with a strand of my damp hair. The gentle touch combined with the soothing rumble of his voice when he comments on the movie has me fighting to keep my eyes open before long.

"Tired, baby?" Jake murmurs against my hair. I just hum drowsily in response, letting my eyes drift shut. I feel Jake shift and then he's gathering me easily in his arms. Too tired to protest being carried, I simply lay my head on his shoulder as he stands and makes his way down the short hall to the bedroom. He lays me gently on the bed, brushing my hair back from my face with a featherlight touch.

"Get some rest darlin'. I'll be right out here on the couch if you need anything." He goes to pull away but my hand darts out to grab his wrist. Our eyes lock and I see the unspoken question there, the line we've been dancing around for days now.

I tug gently and Jake settles on the edge of the mattress. Taking a steadying breath, I caress his bearded cheek.

"Stay. Please." It comes out barely above a whisper but I see his eyes darken in understanding. He knows exactly what I'm asking for. What I want from him tonight.

Jake searches my face, looking for any trace of hesitation or uncertainty. Finding none, he gives a barely perceptible nod and shifts to lay down beside me.

Propped up on one elbow, Jake caresses my face, his rough thumbs tracing my cheekbones reverently. My arms slip around his neck, fingers playing in his hair. He dips his head and he brushes his lips over mine. It's achingly tender at first, both of us taking our time to explore and relearn one another. His fingers trail down my throat, along my collarbone, so feather-light it makes me shiver.

I let my hands wander across the hard planes of his chest, taking in the strength now tempered by his soft touch. Jake's lips leave mine to trail hot, wet kisses down my jaw to my neck. His teeth gently scrape against my skin, sending tingles down my spine.

I arch into him, begging for more as he slides down to nuzzle between my breasts. I feel awkwardly aware of the slight swell of them visible through the thin material of the shirt. His warm breath fanned across my skin makes me shiver in anticipation.

His mouth closes over a nipple, suckling roughly through the fabric. The foreign sensation elicits a moan from me before he lifts his head and I gasp for air. Jake smirks before removing my panties. He then grabs the hem of my shirt, pulling it over my head with almost predatory intent.

The coolness of the room hits my overheated skin, making me shiver. Jake's lips find mine once more, possessive and demanding, and I melt back against the pillows. He lets out a groan into the kiss, one that tells me he's missed this as much as I have.

My fingers tangle in his hair as he pulls off his sweatpants and boxers, freeing him from any more barriers between us. His skin is hot to the touch, and I can't wait to feel every inch of him pressing into me. He rolls onto his back, inviting me to straddle him.

My movements are slow and deliberately sensual as I grind down onto his hips. He groans at the contact, both hands coming up to cup my ass, pulling me down against him. The heat of his cock against me sends a wave of need spiraling through me. I reach down and spread my folds, rubbing the head of his cock through my arousal and over my clit. Our hips begin to move in sync, our gasps and moans echoing off the walls. I lean down to kiss along his jaw, tasting the saltiness from his sweat.

"Fuck," he curses against my lips, voice thick with desire. "You keep doin' that and you're gonna make me lose it."

I smile against him, kissing the hollow of his neck. "Is that okay?" I whisper.

"I'm tryin to let you lead, baby. I want this to be what you want. What you're comfortable with."

"I want you inside me, Jake," I say softly. He nods against my lips, silently telling me he understands.

"Sarah...tell me to stop if you need me to." His words come out strained, like it pains him to even offer that option. But his restraint for my sake only intensifies the want and desire coursing through me.

I silence him with a searing kiss, whispering against his lips, "I don't want you to stop, Jake. I need this...I need you."

He helps me line up his cock at my entrance before pushing in slowly. We both moan at the intimate stretch. My walls clench around him as he thrusts himself into me, filling me completely. My fingers dig into his shoulders as I ride him slowly, savoring the fullness and the feeling of being one with him.

His hands grip my hips tightly, pulling me closer, driving in deeper with each thrust. His mouth moves to my jaw again, biting gently as he takes control of our rhythm. It's both rough and tender, leaving love bites on my skin as he claims me like no one else ever has. We pick up speed, our breathing growing heavy and ragged.

"Sarah," he groans, his voice rough with desire. "You're so fucking tight, baby." I moan in response, unable to speak past the wave of pleasure crashing over me. "Yeah, baby. That's it... that's my good girl."

The soft praise sends shivers down my spine. Heat pools in the place where our bodies connect, intensifying the sensations ravaging my body.

I lean down to kiss him properly. My walls pulse around him and I feel his hips jerk into me harder. I ride him harder, faster.

"Fuck... I'm so close," he growls against my lips. His hand moves to cup my breast, plucking a nipple roughly, sending shockwaves of pleasure through me. His other hand squeezes my ass, pulling me down harder onto his cock as I feel him pulsing inside me.

"Jake!" I cry out as waves of pleasure crash over me.

He thrusts up into me once more and follows with a groan. We stay locked together for long moments, catching our breath before rolling onto our sides and holding each other tightly. Jake's arms wrap around me protectively, both of us still breathing heavily.

We cling to one another as our heartbeats gradually slow, trading tender kisses and caresses, limbs entwined. I've never felt so content and whole before. So utterly safe in another's arms. Jake is my shelter, my soft place to land. With him, I'm finally home.

CHAPTER 13

Sarah

The next few days pass in blissful domesticity. Mornings snuggled together lazily in bed before reluctantly parting ways to start our work days. Evenings spent cooking meals side by side, or having dinner with Marlene, talking easily about anything and everything. Nights wrapped in each other's arms, both of us reluctant to let the other slip from our embrace even in sleep.

Saturday morning arrives and I awake to pale sunlight streaming through the blinds and the smell of coffee brewing. I reach across the bed but find Jake's side empty. I hear faint clattering in the kitchen and smile to myself. My stomach gives a noisy grumble, reminding me I'm eating for two these days.

I slip out of bed and pull on Jake's discarded t-shirt from last night, forgoing pants. Padding quietly out to the kitchen, I find Jake standing at the stove making pancakes, hair still mussed from sleep. He's shirtless, relaxed sweatpants riding low on his hips. I take a moment just to admire the sight of this gorgeous man cooking breakfast in his kitchen.

Jake glances over his shoulder when I step up behind him, slipping my arms around his waist. "Mornin' beautiful," he murmurs, twisting to give me a syrupy sweet kiss. "Made your favorite - chocolate chip pancakes."

"You spoil me, you know that?" I squeeze him affectionately

before moving to grab plates. Jake swats my backside playfully in passing and laughs when I shoot him a cheeky grin over my shoulder. Easy flirtation comes so easily with him.

We sit snuggled close together on the small sofa, legs draped across each other's laps as we enjoy our breakfast. Between bites, Jake reminds me about the town's big spring festival today that he invited me to.

"Beau and a few of the others from the club will have a booth there for the fundraiser barbecue. Thought it'd be a nice way for you to meet everyone. Only if you're feeling up to it though."

The idea of going somewhere public in a crowded setting makes my stomach flip anxiously. I take a slow sip of orange juice to mask my hesitation. "That sounds really nice. I'd love to meet your family."

Jake searches my face, reading me easily. He takes my hand, brushing his thumb over my knuckles soothingly. "It's gonna be ok, Sarah. I'll be with you the whole time."

The sincerity in his steel gray eyes helps settle my nerves somewhat. I trust Jake to keep me safe, even from my own inner demons if need be. Knowing he'll be right by my side makes the apprehension more manageable. I nod, managing a small but genuine smile for him.

"What time do you need to be there to help set up?"

"In a few hours probably." His warm hand comes up to cup my jaw, tilting my face to meet his. "But right now, I just want to spend the morning loving on my girl, if she's up for it." His lips find that sensitive spot below my ear and I melt into him, breakfast forgotten.

Some time later we finally drag ourselves out of bed to get ready. I take a quick shower while Jake packs up the truck with the supplies for the barbecue booth. The hot water sluicing over my skin takes the edge off the anxiety trying to creep back in at the thought of being in such a crowded public place today.

I stand wrapped in a towel staring at my limited clothing options for far too long considering it's just a casual outdoor event. Eventually I settle on a flowy floral sundress that's femme but not overly revealing, with my denim jacket over top. I leave my hair down in soft curls to frame my face.

"Alright, ready when you are babe." Jake leans against the bathroom doorway looking unfairly handsome in just a black t-shirt that strains across his chest, his leather kutte, and faded jeans. I smooth my hands over my dress, taming imaginary wrinkles.

"Is this ok? I don't want to embarrass you."

Jake pushes off the doorframe and moves towards me, hands coming to rest on my hips.

"You look beautiful darlin'. Pretty sure I'm the luckiest bastard alive. I will never be anything but proud to call you mine and have you by my side."

◆ ◆ ◆

The ride into town is a short one, but I can't deny the butterflies fluttering anxiously in my belly as we get closer. I absently smooth my hands over my dress again, taking a few centering breaths.

Sensing my unease, Jake reaches over the center console to squeeze my hand.

"You sure you're up for this? We can just turn around, pick up takeout, have a quiet night in if you want."

His thoughtfulness makes me smile despite my nerves. I bring his hand up to my lips, kissing his knuckles. "I'm ok, promise. I want to meet everyone."

We pull into the park where the festival is being held, trucks and tents already dotting the sprawling grassy field. The sun is out shining brightly, a perfect spring day. Families are arriving in droves, excited children skipping about clutching balloons. My anxiety eases seeing just how welcoming and community oriented the atmosphere feels.

Jake hops out and grabs the folding table from the truck bed while I collect the boxes of miscellaneous supplies. Across the field I spot a large rectangular tent with the Rebel Sons MC logo printed across it. A handful of people are busy setting up tables and grills underneath.

"There they are. Are you ready to meet the crew?" Jake asks with an encouraging smile. Taking his hand, I let him lead us across the grass.

As we approach, a booming voice calls out, "Jake! Over here, son. It's about time you show up."

A tall, barrel chested man, early 50's maybe, with a neatly trimmed salt and pepper beard strides over. His handsome face splits into a wide, infectious grin that instantly puts me at ease. He engulfs Jake in an affectionate bear hug complete with a few hearty claps on the back. When he releases Jake, his eyes land on me.

"Well hey there pretty lady. Jake, you gonna introduce me to your lovely date here or just keep her all to yourself?"

Jake slips an arm around my waist, drawing me close to his side.

"Beau, I'd like you to meet Sarah. Sarah, this here's my Uncle Beau. He's Rex's dad and our club president."

"It's so nice to meet you, Sir." I offer my hand but Beau waves it off, pulling me into a warm hug instead.

"Ain't no need for formalities here, sweetheart. Any special lady in Jake's life is special in ours. Now tell me, how'd this jackass manage to reel in a catch like you?"

I laugh, already charmed by Jake's charismatic uncle. Over Beau's shoulder I see Rex and another younger man approaching. The younger guy claps Jake on the back good naturedly while Rex hangs back a bit more reserved.

"Sarah, this is my brother Wyatt. He wouldn't have been much older than 8 or 9 the last time you saw him. Wyatt is a member of the Rebel Sons, and works at Rigg's Bail & Bounty. He helps out at my shop too. I'm teaching him how to do some of the fabrication on the custom builds. You met our cousin Rex before at the Ridge, he's the club's VP."

Wyatt shakes my hand while Rex offers a polite nod. His sharp eyes seem to study me curiously for a moment but he doesn't say much.

I can't help but burst into laughter when I notice all three men are wearing aprons with different sayings on them. Beau's is the most modest, simply stating 'Mr. Good Lookin' is Cookin'. Rex's apron reads, 'Get a load of Daddy's Meat', and Wyatt's boldly proclaims, 'My meat is 100% going in your mouth today'.

As we all laugh together, I jokingly tease Jake about not wearing an apron. To everyone's surprise, Rex grabs an apron from the table behind him and tosses it to Jake.

"Here you go, cupcake. We ordered this just for you."

Jake unfolds the apron with curiosity, wondering what could be on it. Excitedly, I urged him to put it on and show us. With a smile, Jake ties the apron around his neck and turns to face us, revealing the words 'I rub my own meat'. As we all burst into laughter once again, I look over at Rex and Wyatt with a mischievous grin.

Wyatt gives a nonchalant shrug and replies, "Well, it was true before you came along." With that, he turns and heads towards the grills. Rex bursts into boisterous laughter and trails behind Wyatt.

"Here babe, let me take those." Jake grabs the supply boxes from my arms. "You go on and have a seat, just gonna help the guys get set up."

I settle at one of the picnic tables in the shade with a bottle of water while the Riggs men arrange the grills and get the food prep station set up. More people begin milling around the area as noon approaches. The mouthwatering aroma of burgers and barbecue chicken on the grill soon fills the air.

Despite the growing crowd, I'm feeling surprisingly content with people watching under the sun, chatting with Wyatt and Beau as they work. The constant buzz of activity and laughter makes it easy to blend in unnoticed. And I can see Jake grilling just a few yards away if I need to catch his eye.

Around mid afternoon things are in full swing. I wander through the vendor stalls munching on the loaded hotdog Jake brought me, bobbing my head to the live folk band on stage. Everyone seems to be having a great time. No one pays me much mind as I meander through alone. For the first time in months I feel something akin to normalcy.

Amid the sounds of music and the hustle and bustle, I spot Jake leaning against the truck, watching me with a smile. He's wiping his hands on his apron as he makes his way over, his blue gaze warming my soul.

Before I can say anything, he scoops me up into his strong arms and carries me to the shade of the Riggs tent.

"I thought you might need a break from all this chaos." We giggle as he kisses my nose before settling me down on his lap. "You look so happy here, baby." His voice is thick with pride.

"I am," I say quietly, resting my head against him. "For the first time since... since I can remember."

"That's all I ever want for you, Sarah. For you to find happiness." His impossibly soft lips trail down my neck, his warm breath tickling my ear. "I got you now, and that's all that matters."

Jake keeps his fingers laced with mine as we make our way through the festival grounds. I let Jake lead me around trying our hand at some of the games along the row of booths.

At the ring toss, Jake wins a giant plush teddy bear for me with a bit of good-natured smack talk to the carnie running the game.

"For the little one," he says with a wink, tucking the stuffed bear under his arm.

We share a funnel cake, powdered sugar coating both our faces. Jake pulls me in for a sweet kiss, laughing into my lips.

As darkness falls, we stake out a spot on a grassy hill to watch the fireworks. Jake reclines back on his elbows and I nestle between his bent knees, enveloped in his warmth and strength.

The first boom and crackle makes me jump. Jake's chest rumbles with laughter behind me.

"I got you, baby," he murmurs, dropping a kiss to the top of my head. He absently rubs gentle circles on my belly and I lean back into him, feeling impossibly content.

The grand finale erupts in a riot of glittering light and thunderous bangs. Cheers sound out across the crowd. I turn my face up to see Jake already gazing down at me, eyes glinting in the smoky aftermath.

"Have I told you how amazing you are?" he asks, tucking a strand of hair behind my ear.

I shake my head, suddenly shy. His lips find mine and my heart stutters. I dissolve into the kiss, the rest of the world fading away until it's just us two under the brilliant stars.

On the drive back to his place, his fingers entwined with mine, Jake breaks the comfortable silence.

"You know I'm fallin' for you, Sarah. Fallin' hard," he says quietly.

My breath catches at the admission. I bring our joined hands to my lips, brushing a kiss over his knuckles.

"I'm falling for you too, Jake. I didn't think I could feel this way again, but you make me believe in second chances."

His answering smile rivals the dazzling fireworks display. This remarkable man has awakened my damaged heart, coaxing me back to life. And I can't imagine anywhere I'd rather be than right here by his side.

CHAPTER 14

Jake

Monday morning arrives bright and early. I toss back the sheet and climb out of bed, scrubbing a hand over my beard with a grunt. Rolling my shoulders to work out the kinks, I pad into the small kitchen to start the coffee.

While it brews I hop in the shower, letting the hot spray wash away the last remnants of sleep. I take my time under the water, knowing I've got plenty of time before I need to pick Sarah up.

My mind drifts to her without any conscious thought, like it's just become second nature now. I wonder if she's sleeping ok, if the morning sickness has been bad. I make a mental note to grab some ginger ale and crackers for her when we stop for gas later.

Toweling off and giving my hair a quick comb, I swipe the fog from the steamy mirror. Staring at my reflection, I scrub a hand over my chin critically. Maybe I should clean up this mountain man scruff before our appointment. Make myself a little more presentable to be at Sarah's side for this.

Shaving kit in hand I wipe the condensation from the glass again. Angling my jaw, I begin scraping away the overgrowth methodically until my face is smooth. After a splash of subtle cologne, I give myself a final once over.

I just want Sarah to look at me and feel proud to have me with her today. For her to know without a doubt that I'm one hundred percent committed to her and her child.

In the bedroom I dress in dark jeans and a black button down, rolling the sleeves to my elbows. Casual but pulled together. On my way to grab my boots, I pause in the doorway of the second bedroom. It's sparse, just used mainly for storage right now. But in a few months, hopefully it'll be a nursery.

The crib can go along that wall. She'll need a rocking chair, changing table. My lips quirk thinking of Sarah standing in here holding our little one.

I shake my head, reigning in my thoughts before they run away from me. *Don't go picking out names and building the crib just yet, Riggs. Take it one step at a time.*

Downing the last of my coffee, I pull on my kutte and do a final check that I've got my wallet, keys, and phone before heading out the door. Despite my attempts to appear cool and collected, my palms are sweating against the worn leather steering wheel. I'm nervous as hell about today, but I don't want Sarah sensing that. She's already got enough stress and anxiety without my nerves adding to it.

As soon as I put the truck in park, the back door of the B&B swings open and Gram steps out onto the porch. She's got a steaming mug clutched in her hands and a warm smile on her face.

"Mornin' dear! Come on inside. I just brewed a fresh pot of coffee if you'd like some."

I accept the offer, following her inside the cozy little inn. The kitchen smells like cinnamon and cloves, and something tasty just came out of the oven judging by the heat still lingering in the air.

Gram busies herself prepping a tray with mugs, cream, and sugar while I lean against the butcher block island.

"So today's the big day, huh? How're you feeling?" Gram asks.

I rub at the back of my neck, trying to play it cool even though my stomach is in knots. "Oh you know, just hoping everything looks good with the baby."

Marlene gives me an appraising look over her glasses, like she can see right through my false bravado. Her expression softens knowingly.

"It's ok to be anxious, Jake. First appointments are always nerve-wracking, especially for first-time dads."

I just chuckle softly, touched that this kind-hearted woman already considers me the father of Sarah's child when biologically, I'm not. But I aim to change that as soon as Sarah will let me.

"Sarah's just about ready upstairs. Nerves are getting to the poor thing I'm afraid, though she tries not to show it." Gram fixes her own cup before taking the seat across from me.

I nod, wrapping my palm around the mug, hoping to disguise the faint tremor of my own anxiety. "I figured as much. She's been through more than anyone should ever have to. I can't blame her for feeling unsure and overwhelmed by all this."

Gram pats my hand knowingly. "Oh Honey, every first time mama feels that way, even under the best of circumstances. What's important is that she knows she's not alone anymore. That little one already has you wrapped around their tiny fingers and you haven't even met yet," she says with a conspiratorial wink.

I duck my head with a laugh, knowing there's no point trying to deny it. This child - mine or not biologically - has already carved out a place in my heart. The possibility of a family with Sarah, of being a father, feels like the missing piece I never knew was lacking in my life.

Soft footsteps on the stairs draw our attention. I stand automatically when Sarah appears in the kitchen doorway. She's worrying her bottom lip, but damn if she still isn't the most breathtaking sight I've ever seen. Her long dark hair falls softly around her shoulders, and she manages a small smile despite the obvious nerves swirling behind those green eyes I adore.

"Hey there, darlin', ready to get going?"

"You clean up real nice," Sarah says with a hint of teasing to her voice now. Her hands smooth down my chest appreciatively and I grin.

"I thought I should try to make myself presentable for our big appointment today."

Sarah's nose scrunches up adorably. "I like the scruffy look too though. Makes you look all dangerous and sexy." Her boldness takes me by surprise and I bark out a laugh.

"Oh trust me Darlin', that look ain't goin' anywhere. Just thought I'd try to rein it in for the doctor's office." With one last quick peck to her lips I take her hand to lead her out to the truck, eager to get this show on the road.

Gram's voice stops me before we make it two steps. "Hold on now! I need a picture of you two to commemorate the big day." She's waving her phone at us eagerly.

Sarah tries to politely decline but Gram is having none of it. "Oh hush now, it'll just take a second." She gestures us closer together in front of the big bay windows drenching us in warm morning sunlight.

Unable to say no to Gram's insistent mothering, I wrap my arms around Sarah, holding her close to my side. She snakes her arm around my back, hand curving over my hip. Our bodies fit together like two puzzle pieces.

Sarah tilts her face up to me just as Gram gives an excited

"Perfect!" and the telltale artificial camera click sounds from her phone.

"Beautiful! Now you two get on out of here before you're late." Gram makes little shooing motions with her hands.

With final farewells and well wishes from Gram, Sarah and I head out to the truck hand in hand. Sarah lets out a shaky breath once she's settled in the passenger seat and her seatbelt clicks into place. She fidgets anxiously with the worn cuff of her sweater, gaze fixed out the window on the forests and ranches speeding by. I slide my palm over to rest on her knee, just offering a small reassuring touch.

"So I was thinkin' after your appointment, maybe we could stop and get lunch somewhere if you're feelin' up to it. Or we could do some shopping over in Mason, hit up the big department stores they don't have here in North Ridge."

Sarah turns towards me, lips quirking up. "Trying to distract me, huh?"

I grin sheepishly, caught red-handed. "Maybe a little. Is it working?"

"A little," she admits with an affectionate eye roll. Her slender fingers cover mine where they rest on her leg, thumb stroking over my scarred knuckles. I'm struck once again by how perfectly her small hand fits in mine.

The silence settles over us once more as we get closer to our destination, but it's a comfortable one. My earlier apprehension has faded now that it's just me and my girl.

The Mason Women's Health Clinic comes into view about 45 minutes later. It's newer construction, clean lines of glass and steel nestled between rows of sturdy oak trees just off the highway. A far cry from the cramped single practitioner's office back home in North Ridge that sees most of the residents.

Taking her hand, I help her down from the truck and keep my arm wrapped securely around her waist as we head inside.

The clinic waiting area is brightly lit with walls painted a muted sage green color. Soothing instrumental spa music plays quietly in the background. A large fish tank bubbles away in the corner. The tranquil atmosphere seems designed to put anxious expectant mothers at ease.

Sarah stays tucked close to my side while we check in at the front desk and fill out a mountain of paperwork. She pauses at the line asking for patient name, biting her lip nervously. Right. She can't exactly use her legal name in case word got back to that bastard somehow.

I squeeze her shoulder, keeping my voice low and calm. "Just put down whatever name you want, darlin'. If your OK with it, I'd like you to put me down as the father and I'll give them my insurance info so the baby will be covered."

Sarah thinks for a moment then neatly prints 'Sarah Riggs' in the name field. My last name. The significance isn't lost on me and I have to quickly turn my head before she sees my eyes glaze over. I discreetly wipe at them, passing it off as an itch while I fill in my personal and insurance details. By the time we turn the forms back in, you'd never know anything was amiss looking at them. The receptionist doesn't bat an eye.

In the waiting room, I keep a protective arm around Sarah's shoulders as we sit crammed together on a tiny loveseat. She's back to fidgeting, heels tapping anxiously against the linoleum. I cover her knee with my big palm, stroking my thumb slowly back and forth in what I hope is a soothing motion.

After what feels like an eternity, a nurse finally steps through the door and calls out "Sarah Riggs?"

I stand when Sarah does but hang back an uncertain step, not wanting to overstep or assume my presence is wanted beyond the waiting room.

"You want me to come with you, darlin'?" I ask gently. *Please say yes, please say yes.*

Sensing my hesitation, Sarah reaches back and twines her delicate fingers through mine, giving a light tug. "C'mon, daddy," she says with a playful quirk of her lips that makes my heart damn near burst. Unable to stop grinning like a fool, I let her lead me back to the exam room.

The perky nurse, Amanda according to her ID badge, leads us down a short hallway dotted with framed nature photography. She shows us into the first exam room on the right. My eyes roam curiously over the space. It's smaller than I expected but still manages to feel homey rather than sterile. A scale and blood pressure machine occupy one corner. An exam table sits centered below informational pregnancy and anatomy posters on the walls. A rolling stool and medical cart take up the remaining space.

The nurse weighs and measures Sarah, takes her vitals, and asks her a few questions about her last monthly cycle and general health. I stay right by Sarah's side the whole time.

"You must be Daddy, congratulations! I'm so glad you could join us today. We just love getting the whole family involved." I offer a polite smile and nod.

"Yes ma'am. I'm Jake. This is my..." My throat unexpectedly thickens. Sarah isn't technically mine yet, even though I want her to be. I clear my throat awkwardly. "I'm real excited to be here today."

If she picks up on my verbal stumbling, Amanda gives no indication. She's already redirecting her attention to Sarah, asking questions in a friendly but professional manner.

"And is this your first baby as well, Dad?"

"Oh I'm not actually..." I falter, uncertain how exactly to define my role here. Sarah squeezes my hand.

"Yes," Sarah inserts gently, "this will be the first for both of us."

Amanda nods easily, not pressing for more details.

"Well congratulations to you both! Now the doctor will be in shortly to get started with a quick ultrasound to get some measurements and confirm dates."

The doctor enters the room with a warm and welcoming smile, immediately making us feel comfortable. She goes over the paperwork, asking Sarah questions to confirm details about her medical history.

Finally, the doctor rolls over the ultrasound machine. The paper liner crinkles as Sarah reclines back and slips her feet into the stirrups. I keep my eyes locked on hers as the doctor explains what she's doing during the exam. I can't resist glancing over when the telltale thump of a heartbeat suddenly fills the small room.

My vision goes blurry, unshed tears making the image on the screen swim before me. That's our baby's heartbeat. Our child, our future. The doctor says some things about the due date that I vaguely register as November 11th, and that Sarah is 10 weeks. But all I can focus on is the thump-thump-thump and Sarah's hand clutched tightly in mine.

When the exam is finished and Sarah is cleaned up, we reluctantly break contact so she can slide off the table. I immediately wrap my arm around her shoulders again, pressing a fierce kiss to her temple. I don't trust my voice not to break right now so I just smile down at her, hoping she can read the emotion and promises in my eyes. From this moment on, I will move heaven and earth for her and our baby.

The receptionist is preoccupied when we first exit the exam

room, engrossed in something on her computer screen. As we approach the desk, her eyes lift and instantly widen in recognition.

"Jake? Jake Riggs?" The leggy blonde comes around from behind the desk, ignoring Sarah to focus her attention solely on me. A coy smile plays on her artificially plumped lips.

"Wow it's been ages! What are you doing here?" Her overly friendly tone and the way her gaze roams over me sets me on edge. *Does she not see my arm around the pregnant woman beside me?*

I keep my tone clipped, offering only a polite nod. "Hey Carrie. Just had an appointment for the baby." I emphasize the last word and tighten my hold on Sarah's shoulders meaningfully. Message received, Carrie's eyes flick to Sarah briefly before she pastes that fake smile back on.

"Oh how sweet. Well it was nice running into you, Jakey." I have to stop myself from visibly cringing at the nickname. "We'll have to catch up sometime."

"Take care, Carrie," I mutter, already steering Sarah towards the exit before she can toss out any more thinly veiled invitations. The doors can't swing shut fast enough behind us.

Sarah is quiet on the walk back to the truck, arms crossed protectively over her middle. I open her door and help her up into the cab, but once I'm behind the wheel, the tension is palpable. I reach over to cover her hand with mine, hating the hurt I see clouding her pretty features.

"Darlin', you know she didn't mean anything to me, right? Carrie was just an old mistake, long before you came back into my life. It was never even close to what me and you have."

Sarah shrugs half-heartedly but won't meet my eyes. I gently turn her face towards mine.

"I haven't wanted anyone else since the day you walked back into my life. That isn't going to change as long as I have you. You and this little one are my whole world now."

I talk to Sarah honestly about my history with Carrie on the drive home. Emphasizing it never went beyond the physical, and I haven't seen or spoken to her in almost a year.

By the time we cross back into North Ridge, the easy affection and laughter between me and Sarah returns. Her smile and trust are the only things that matter to me now.

When we get to my place, I open the truck door for her and help her climb out. Looking down at her, "So… you call me daddy now, huh?"

Sarah is grinning shyly, "Yeah, I like the sound of it," she confesses softly.

My answering smile feels wide enough to split my face in two. I cup her jaw, swiping my thumb over the apple of her cheek. "Yeah?"

Her grin turns impish, green eyes dancing. "Mmhmm… daddy."

I groan and crush my lips to hers again, the teasing little minx. She laughs against my mouth, kissing me back for a few more blissful moments before finally slipping past me into the trailer.

I send Sarah to shower and change into something comfortable while I whip up an early dinner. I fire up the grill out back and throw on a couple steaks I had marinating. While they sizzle away, I chop up stuff for a salad and get some mac and cheese in the oven.

By the time Sarah emerges, hair damp and wearing that sexy little tank top that hugs her curves, I've got dinner plated and waiting on the coffee table by the sofa.

During dinner, Sarah brings up her ultrasound today,

mentioning how I seemed both excited and nervous. I put down my plate and grabbed both of her hands. Our eyes locked, and I finally admitted, "I have always wanted to be a dad," I confessed. "And after seeing that precious little life on the screen today, hearing its heartbeat, I want it more than anything." My words hung in the air as Sarah looked at me with tears in her eyes. "I know I'm not this baby's biological father," I said, "but if you'll let me, I would really like to be this baby's dad. I will love and protect that child no differently than I would if they were my own."

Sarah's eyes shimmer behind a sheen of unshed tears as she launches herself into my lap, arms hugged tightly around my neck.

"Of course I want you to be our baby's father, Jake," she whispers fiercely against my cheek. "We're going to be a family."

I just cling to my two favorite people, unable to speak past the massive lump in my throat. Sarah wants me to be her child's father.

We stay locked together, just holding one another close until Sarah pulls back, caressing my cheeks tenderly. The emotion shining in her eyes mirrors my own. Without a word, I stand and sweep her up securely in my arms, carrying her down the short hall to my bedroom. I sit down on the mattress, Sarah's body straddling mine. Our lips meet again and again, tenderly reaffirming the promises and future unfolding before us.

"It's like we were always meant to end up here, Sarah. No matter what bad we had to go through to get here, I promise it's going to be nothing but good from here on." I whisper against her lips as I deepen the kiss, my strong arms wrapping around her curvy frame.

Sarah melts into me, her softness contrasting with my hard muscles. The scent of her shampoo mixed with something more, something uniquely hers that makes me so damn hard for her.

My hands roam her supple skin, tracing down to cup her ass and bring her up to grind against my cock. She gasps into my mouth and I take it as an invitation to continue. Her need mirrors mine as we undress each other eagerly, discarding clothes on the floor in haste.

She steps out of her panties and pulls me close again, our naked bodies pressing tightly together. I lay her down gently on the mattress, taking in every inch of her body. My woman's body is a masterpiece, every curve and line carefully crafted to perfection. Her skin is warm and inviting, soft to the touch under my rough hands. Her hips are wide and welcoming, her thighs thick and lush. And her round, plump ass is a sight to behold. Her gorgeous round tits are just begging for my attention. But what I love the most is her soft stomach growing my child.

My mouth finds one erect nipple, sucking softly as I trail kisses down her body. When I reach the apex of her thighs, she parts them eagerly, inviting me inside. My fingers brush against her swollen clit before slipping inside her wet heat, groaning at how ready she is for me. I lick my fingers, tasting her, and then plunge them deep into her core. Her back arches off the mattress as she cries out my name, liquid heat coating my fingers. This woman – this amazing broken angel – is mine again.

I suck and lick at her clit while pumping my fingers, rubbing her g spot. I hear her moans, see her body trembling under me, and know I'm the only one who can make her feel this way. It drives me wild. She cries out again as she comes undone, her walls gripping tight around my fingers. I slide another finger inside of her, stretching her while she shudders against me.

I replace my fingers with my cock, sliding in slow and steady, feeling her delicious, wet, heat surround me like a second skin. She closes her eyes and bites her bottom lip, throwing her head back in pleasure as I begin to thrust into her.

"Fuck, Sarah," I breathe against her shoulder, "you're so fucking sexy."

Her nails rake down my back as she takes my cock, meeting every stroke, taking everything I have to give. The smell of sex and sweat mingles in the air, mixing with the taste of her on my tongue. Our moans fill the room as we fuck like it's been years since we've been with one another instead of days. My hands grip her hips tightly when I feel that tiny tremor of release deep inside her.

"Come for me, baby," I say against her ear, and she does just that, her cries of my name echoing off the walls as she comes again. "That's it baby, good girl. I love watching you come on my cock."

I follow close behind, groaning deeply into her neck as I empty myself within her. The mattress creaks under our combined weight as I collapse on top of her, panting against her skin.

She kisses my chest, smiling up at me. "I love you, Jake." she whispers softly, and it feels like the greatest victory of my life.

"I love you too Darlin'."

As I drift off to sleep later that night, with Sarah's body spooned to mine and our child nestled between us, I know this is where I'm meant to be: protecting them both from anything, or anyone that threatens them.

CHAPTER 15

Michael

I sit brooding in my home office, staring at the photos of Sarah pinned to the corkboard on the wall. She's everywhere - Sarah smiling on our wedding day, Sarah cooking dinner, Sarah asleep in our bed. My fist slams down on the heavy wooden desk, sending a pen clattering to the floor. How dare she defy me. After everything I've done for her, given her. This is how the cunt repays me? By running away in the middle of the night like a coward?

"The bitch will pay for this," I mutter under my breath. "No one makes a fool of Michael Moretti."

I'm so consumed by rage, I don't hear the heavy footsteps on the stairs. My father's gruff voice startles me from my brooding.

"Still moping around up here, are you?" Tony Moretti scoffs from the office doorway, meaty arms crossed over his barrel chest. "I told you that pretty little wife of yours was trouble the first time I laid eyes on her."

I scowl, shoving away from the desk. "Don't start with me, old man. It's not my fault the ungrateful bitch decided to skip town."

Tony's expression blackens, his hand shooting out to backhand me hard across the face. I stumble back a step, my cheek flaming.

"Watch your mouth, boy. Need I remind you it was my connections that got you that cushy DEA job? My money that paid for that fancy wedding and this house you shared with your traitorous bitch of a wife?" my father steps closer, crowding into my space.

"Thanks to you losing control of her, our entire operation is at risk now. That girl knows too much!" He punctuates this by jabbing two thick fingers into my chest.

I knocked his hand away angrily. "She doesn't know anything. All she knows is I work for the DEA. I've never told her a damn thing about the trafficking of girls, or the drugs. The trafficking was all your idea anyway. I never wanted any part of it. I just went along with it to get you off my fucking back."

Tony barks out a harsh laugh. "Is that what you tell yourself so you can sleep at night? Face it boy, you're a Moretti through and through. It's in your blood."

I turn away, raking a hand through my dark hair. I hate how he can push my buttons and get under my skin so easily, even now.

Taking a deep breath, I turn back. "Look, it's not my fault Sarah got it in her head to rabbit on me. But I'll find her and fix this. I always do."

Tony's eyes narrow, his tone laced with warning. "For both your sakes, you better pray that wife of yours keeps her pretty little mouth shut about our business."

I wave this off impatiently. "She won't talk. Sarah's too scared of me to try anything. She knows what I'm capable of." A sinister smile curves my lips.

Tony scoffs. "Don't get cocky. That girl grew a spine and left your ass, didn't she?"

I slam my father back against the oak paneled wall, my forearm pressed to his throat.

"Don't forget who you're talking to, old man," I growl. "I've got this under control."

Tony shoves me off, straightening his rumpled suit jacket.

"See that you do, and do it quickly. If I have to step in there will be consequences, my boy. For both of you. I'll be at the office. Get your shit together, and handle your business like a man so I can go back east."

With that ominous threat left swirling in his wake, my father descends the stairs again. I wait until I hear the front door slam shut before sweeping my arm across the desk violently, sending everything crashing to the floor. Worthless old bastard. I'll show him just how in control Michael Moretti can be.

Starting over from scratch won't be easy, but I've never backed down from a challenge before. There are still moves to make, leads to follow. Sarah was clever, covering her tracks. But everyone slips up eventually, and her slip up was Anna. You never leave anyone alive who can talk.

Grabbing my keys, I decide to make a trip down to see an old "friend" of the family. Bruno runs a chop shop on the south side that also doubles as a hub for Moretti's trafficking ring. The operation is small potatoes compared to Tony's grand visions, just moving desperate girls in from the streets, sometimes other countries, before sending them down the coast to the selling block. But it's profitable, and Bruno's proven his loyalty over the years.

The smell of motor oil and grease hits my nose as soon as I step from the car. The garage is eerily quiet, none of the usual revving engines or power tools ringing out. I pass through the workshop to the office, towards the back corner where I know the entrance to the basement is hidden.

As expected, I find Bruno and a couple of his thugs sitting around an old card table nursing beers. Bruno starts, hurriedly rising to his feet.

"Mr. Moretti! We weren't expecting you today." The thugs shuffle nervously, exchanging glances. I ignore them, dropping down into Bruno's recently vacated chair and propping my feet up on the table casually.

"Relax Bruno, this isn't an official visit. I just need some information, and I think you're the man who can get it for me."

Bruno visibly relaxes at this, taking a seat across from me. "Of course, anything you need, boss."

I lean forward, elbows braced on the table. "I need everything your contacts can dig up on my wife Sarah's whereabouts. Friends she might reach out to, places she might go. There's got to be a paper trail somewhere we can follow."

Bruno scratches at his salt and pepper stubble thoughtfully. "I'll put the word out tonight. Tap into my informants around the city, maybe even up the coast. We'll find her for you boss, don't you worry. A pretty little thing like your Sarah can't stay hidden for long."

I sit back with a satisfied smile. "Good man. Knew I could count on you." I slide an expensive cigar across the table to Bruno who accepts it eagerly.

While I wait on Bruno's contacts to start funneling in information, I decide to pay a visit to another one of the basements new occupants. She's proven useful in gaining intel from Sarah in the past.

I make my way down the gloomy hallway to the last room on the left. I unlock the heavy door and step inside, wrinkling my nose at the dank air. Well, my guest will just have to cope. Comfort is a privilege, not a right, as I frequently remind her.

At the sound of the door, the room's sole occupant sits up on the dingy little cot wedged in the corner. Dark curls spill over her shoulders as she shrinks back against the wall, watching me warily.

I force a smile that feels more like a leer. "There's my girl. Did you miss me, Anna?"

She says nothing, merely wraps her arms around herself tighter. I tsk as I approach the bed slowly.

"Now now, that's no way to greet your dear brother. Father would be very disappointed with your poor manners."

At the mention of my father, Anna flinches. Good. She still knows her place.

I sit beside her on the cot, grasping her chin in a painful grip when she tries to turn away.

"I don't have time for your games today, Anna. I need information, and you're going to give it to me. Understand?"

Her dark eyes flash with defiance, but she gives a small jerky nod. I reward her obedience by stroking her hair almost tenderly. I enjoy keeping her off balance like this.

"That's my good girl. Now tell me, did my darling wife confide in you at all before she decided to flee in the night like a gutless coward?"

Anna presses her lips together, remaining silent. I feel my fragile patience fraying. My hand fists in her hair, wrenching her head to the side. She cries out.

"I suggest you answer me. I won't ask nicely again."

When she still refuses to speak, I launch off the cot and begin pacing the small room like a caged animal. "Useless bitch," I seethe under my breath. "Just like all the rest of you ungrateful whores."

I know what I have to do, clearly pain will be the only motivator here. Striding to the door, I call for the guard stationed down the hall to bring me the tools from the closet. The man returns swiftly with the duffel bag, his eyes skittering away uneasily when they land on Anna's huddled form. I dismiss him with a sharp word.

With clinical precision, I begin laying the tools out on the rickety table by the door. Pliers, knives, handcuffs, a coiled whip. Anna's breaths come faster at the sight. *Excellent.*

I pick up the handcuffs first, advancing on her slowly.

"Last chance to make this easy on yourself."

When she stays mute, I grab her wrists and wrench them behind her back, closing the cold metal cuffs tightly. I haul Anna to her feet and drag her into the center of the room beneath the bare hanging lightbulb. I can almost taste her fear now, sharp and acrid on my tongue.

I call for two of the men playing cards to come into the room. "Strip her," I order gruffly. They exchange an uncertain look but comply, avoiding Anna's teary eyes as they methodically remove her clothing. She shivers in just her bra and panties, arms still cuffed behind her back.

I circle her slowly. "You know you deserve this, don't you? All of it. This is what happens to traitorous, lying, bitches. To people who defy me."

Anna shakes her head frantically, dark curls spilling across her shoulders. "P-please Michael..." she whimpers. *Fucking Pathetic.*

I backhand her across the mouth, splitting her lip. "Quiet. You had your chance to talk. Now we do this my way."

I nod to the guards. One of them picks up the coil of rope, binding Anna's feet and calves tightly together. She has to struggle not to lose her balance. The other guard slides a length of rusted pipe through the links of the handcuffs at her back, forcing her arms up at an unnatural angle. Her face twists in pain.

I slowly circle her bound form. I trail the whip almost gently across her thighs and torso. Anna flinches away with a choked sob. The first crack of the whip splits the air, followed by her ragged scream.

Again and again I bring the unforgiving length of braided leather down across her bare skin. Her olive skin splits open, crimson streaking down her trembling body. Still, she refuses to break. Rage and frustration war within me. I want to break her. I need to hear her screams, and see the defiant light leave her eyes.

Grabbing a filthy rag, I gag her roughly, muffling her cries. That's better. Now I can think. Striding to the table, my hand hovers over my tools before selecting a thin sharp blade. Perfect.

I slice the blade slowly down Anna's heaving ribs, just deep enough to bloom red. She jerks against her bonds, gag stifling her screams. Blood trickles steadily from the fresh cut.

Leaning in close to her ear, I whisper, "I can keep going all night, sweetheart. I've only just begun. But it can stop, whenever you want. Just tell me where my wife is."

Anna's eyes are glassy with pain, cheeks slick with tears. But I see it - the exact moment her will breaks. Her shoulders slump in defeat.

I remove the gag, smoothing her hair back gently. "There now, that's better. Time to have our little chat."

Broken, voice raw from screaming, Anna confesses that she helped Sarah plot her escape. Drove her to the bus station in the middle of the night and gave her cash for a ticket. I force Anna to repeat it again and again until every detail is seared into my brain. She helped Sarah, my wife, flee to some backwater town called North Ridge in Montana to stay with an old friend.

Rage explodes through me with the force of a volcanic eruption.

I lash out with my fist, punching a hole straight through the cheap plaster wall. My chest heaves as I struggle to rein myself back under control.

When I turn back, I grasp Anna's face with bloody knuckles, forcing her to meet my wild eyes. "You've been very helpful, sweetheart." My grin is more a baring of teeth. "I think we're done here for today."

I leave her bound and bleeding without a backward glance. Bloody handprints stain the stair railing as I ascend from that dark basement prison. The door to my father's office stands slightly ajar. I shoulder my way inside.

Tony looks up from his desk casually. "Learn anything useful?"

I brace my hands on my father's desk. "I know where she is. I'm going after her."

My father arches one bushy brow. "Oh? And where might that be?"

"Some pissant town in Montana called North Ridge. She's holed up there with an old friend apparently." My lip curls derisively.

Tony steeples his fingers, regarding me shrewdly. "And just how do you propose to get your hands on her clear out in Big Sky Country without drawing suspicion? In case you forgot, you're still a federal agent. Hard to maintain a low profile when you're flashing your badge everywhere."

I scrub a hand down my face. I hate to admit it, but the old bastard has a point.

"I'll take a leave of absence from the bureau. Tell them it's a family emergency."

"They'll want details."

"So I'll give them some," I snap. "Make up a sick relative or some bullshit. I don't care. All I need is enough time to get to Montana and retrieve my wife."

Tony considers me silently. I force myself to stand still beneath that piercing stare. Finally, he nods.

"Very well. Bring her back by any means necessary. Don't screw it up, boy."

A savage smile slowly spreads across my face. Oh, I'll bring Sarah back all right. And she'll pay dearly for every sleepless night and dead end I've suffered chasing after her like an escaped convict. She wants to run and hide? I'll hunt her to the ends of the earth. No one escapes Michael Moretti for long.

Sarah got a head start, but my turn is coming. And this time when I catch her, I won't be letting go again until she's paid tenfold for her betrayal.

The next few days pass in a blur of preparations. I hand off my active case load and file for emergency family leave from the DEA, citing a sick sister back east who needs my help. Just as expected, it's granted without question. Perks of being a seasoned agent with an unblemished record, at least on paper.

I pack light, just the essentials for a long road trip. Most importantly, I pack my lockbox of guns and knives. While I prefer using my fists or just the strength of my own hands, it never hurts to be prepared. This is one hunt I can't afford to screw up.

CHAPTER 16

Jake

My Sarah,

You continue to disappoint me, love. Did you really believe running away like a coward, in the dead of night could sever our bond? You are bound to me forever, the collar around that pretty neck marked with my name.

I found where you've scurried off to, little rabbit. Did you honestly think I would fall for your fucking lies? That a few state lines and a couple hundred miles could keep me from taking what's mine? Our marriage vows were until death do us part. Have you forgotten?

I'm here to reclaim my property, and this time I won't be letting you slip your leash again. You owe me a debt,

Sarah, for all the sleepless nights and dead ends I've endured searching for my cheating whore of a wife. It's time for me to collect.

When I get my hands on you, I will remind you, who you belong to in every possible way, as many times as it takes to break you again. No one else will ever have you, touch you, fuck you. You belong to me, every fucking inch. Your body, your wet mouth, your pussy, all of it is mine to use as I please. I will bind you in ropes and chains, so you never forget this again. Your body is my slave, to do with as I desire. I will brand your soft skin, so everyone knows your claimed property. You will cry and beg so sweetly for mercy, mercy you will not find.

You were foolish to test me, little rabbit. But don't worry, I will teach you obedience once more. This I vow to you. No matter where you try to hide, I will always come for you, to claim what is rightfully mine.

M.M.

I take a seat on the worn, floral couch in the living room of Gram's B&B. My eyes fixed on the letter I hold in my hands. My jaw clenched so tightly it causes pain. I can barely make out the words on the paper through my fury, my pulse thundering in my ears. I can feel rage coursing through my body, clouding my thoughts. The letter trembles slightly as I try to control my anger for Sarah's sake.

I'm going to kill this mother fucker.

Sarah paces back and forth, gnawing anxiously on a thumbnail. I hate seeing her so shaken. She stops suddenly, turning to me with fear pooling in her green eyes.

"What am I going to do, Jake? He found me!" Her voice wavering slightly.

She rushes to me and I fold her into my arms. "It's okay. I've got you now."

Sarah clings to me, her body trembling. "He found me, Jake. I don't know how, but he knows where I am."

"It's alright baby, I won't let him hurt you," I vow, the words both a promise and a prayer. She clings to me tightly, tears wetting my shirt. I've never seen her look so afraid, and it guts me.

I dig my hand into my pocket to find my phone and call Rex. After two rings his familiar voice answers, laid back as ever.

"Jake cuz, what's up?"

"Hey Rex. Listen, I need a favor..." I quickly fill him in on the letter left for Sarah. Rex whistles low under his breath.

"Shit brother, that's fucked up."

I pass a hand over my face tiredly, feeling the stubble scratch against my palm. "I know, we need to lock down Gram's B&B, make sure they are both safe here."

"No doubt, better safe than skull-bashed-in-by-a-psychopath. I can clear my schedule and be there this afternoon to start the install. I'm pretty sure I have enough equipment laying around to install a full system. Motion sensors, cameras, the works."

I glance at my watch, seeing it's only 8:00 a.m. "That'd be great. And listen... there's one more thing. Any chance you can keep an eye out for Moretti's name popping up anywhere? Credit cards, cell phones, anything to indicate if he's been on the move?"

"Way ahead of you brother, I've still got all those alerts running from when we first looked into Moretti a few months back. And speak of the damn devil, I was literally just about to call you. Got a ping early this morning that Moretti's Amex just got swiped. Couple charges out of Montana at a car rental place, some no-name motel, couple gas station charges."

"When exactly did those charges hit?"

"Mm, looks like they are all over the last 48 hours. Guy must've found some intel. Judging by the timestamps, the psycho twat waffle hopped in his car and drove straight through from Oregon only stopping to fuel up."

I scrub a hand through my hair, mind racing. "Alright, thanks man. See you in a few hours."

I end the call and fill Sarah in on Rex's news, softening the edges so I don't spook her further. Still, I can tell his name alone has her panicked.

I catch her hands, squeezing gently until some of the tension bleeds from her shoulders. "Hey, try not to freak yourself out, okay? Rex and I got you. I'll die before I let that bastard anywhere near you again. Now, I have to go into the shop for a few hours and get some work done so I can come back here and help Rex install the security system this afternoon. You're more than welcome to come along with me, I'd prefer it."

"I have to go to work at the Ridge today. I should have been there an hour ago."

"Alright Darlin', I'll drop you off at the Ridge on my way to the shop. You call me if you need anything. I'm two minutes away if you need me. I'll pick you up when I get finished at the shop."

After dropping Sarah off at the Ridge, I head over to my garage. I pull into the lot and a fresh rage ignites inside me. A dead rabbit hanging from the door greets me. The sick fuck cut the rabbits feet off then nailed it to my door, along with a scrap of paper scrawled with a threat:

"You can't keep what doesn't belong to you."

It takes every ounce of willpower not to put my fist through the nearest window. Son of a bitch. He was here, on my doorstep while I slept, and I never even realized it. This wasn't just some pissed off local trying to scare us. This was Moretti, staking his claim. And if he was bold enough to leave me a goddamn calling card, he clearly wasn't intimidated. Yet.

This attack confirms Michael sees me as an obstacle between him and Sarah. Good. The angrier he gets, the more mistakes he'll make. And I'll be waiting for the fucker.

As soon as I had finished cleaning up the mess on the garage door, Beau showed up. He offered to lend a hand and help out with any work around the garage so that I could focus on Sarah, and helping Rex with setting up the security system later in the day.

I'd hardly finished filling Beau in on the welcome gift hanging on my garage door this morning, when my cell phone rings. One look at the caller ID has my adrenaline surging again, it's Sophia. She's practically incoherent, babbling about something hanging on the door to her office. God damnit, he's actively stalking her.

I quickly assure Sophia I'm on my way before hanging up. Beau is already shrugging into his jacket, jaw clenched.

"That psycho's crossed a line. Let's go."

Beau cracks his massive knuckles in agreement, always ready for a fight. The two of us climb onto our bikes and race over to The

Ridge, Beau calling Rex to meet us there.

Sarah practically collapses into my arms the second I step through the back entrance of The Ridge, overflowing with relief at the sight of me. She's pale and shaky, mascara smudged beneath her eyes from crying. But unharmed, thank God.

Beau steps into the kitchen holding what was found nailed to Sophia's office door. Two bloody rabbit feet, one hanging from either end of a piece of twine.

"Son, this note was stuck to the office door with a knife. The feet were hanging from the knife handle." I grab the note from Beau's outstretched hand.

"Nowhere to run, little rabbit."

The violation makes me see red all over again.

Just then Rex comes through the front door of the Ridge. "Hey man, did you notice that black SUV parked across the street? It's facing this way, and it definitely looks like it's not from around here. I've never seen it before. The windows are too dark to see inside."

"No, we came in through the back." I toss out at Rex while walking to the front of the Ridge. A lone black SUV idles at the curb, windows darkened. I turn to Rex and Beau with a whispered order to hang back in case this is it. Then I start casually crossing the street, every muscle coiled tight as tripwire.

As soon as I'm within 20 feet of the suspicious SUV, the engine revs violently. I freeze, hand dropping to the gun holstered at my back just as the tires peel out. The SUV launches straight towards me, intent clear. I throw myself out of the path of the speeding two-ton death machine at the last possible second, hitting the pavement hard.

I'm back up on my feet quickly as the SUV fishtails around the corner, nothing more than a shrinking speck now. But not before I burned every detail of the plate number into my brain. No way that wasn't our guy. The boldness of his attack shakes me, even as fury burns hot under my skin. He'll regret not just running me down when he had the chance.

Rex jogs over, eyes wide. "Shit man, that was close. You get the plate?" At my tight nod he pulls out his phone to run the number. A minute later he looks up, expression grave.

"The SUV is a rental, it was rented yesterday from the same place Moretti's card was charged. Guess this means he's officially crashed our party."

◆ ◆ ◆

Later that night, I'm startled awake by the security alarm blaring from my phone. I leap out of bed, throw on clothes, and race to my truck. The tires spitting gravel as I tear out of the driveway. My hands grip the wheel hard as I speed down the gravel drive. In less than a minute I'm skidding to a stop in the back of the B&B.

I discover a broken window in the kitchen and signs of forced entry. Fear pierces my heart.

"Sarah!" I shout, sweeping through the rooms and finding them empty. Panicked scenarios flood my mind. Did Michael abduct her? Hurt her? Or worse?

"Jake!" Sarah appears at the top of the stairs, wrapped in a robe, eyes wide. "What's happening?"

Relief crashes over me at the sight of her unharmed. I take the stairs two at a time and pull her into my arms. "You're okay. The alarm went off. I thought..."

"I'm fine," she assures me, hugging me back fiercely. "Just rattled. Do you think it was him?"

My jaw clenches. "It was him. But he's gone now. And he's not gettin' his hands on you, I swear it."

Sarah nods against my chest, her frightened trembles subsiding. I keep holding her tight.

"Baby, can you do me a favor and go check on Gram while I clean up this glass and find something to cover the broken window until I can replace it tomorrow?"

As I finish securing the window for the night, Gram and Sarah enter the kitchen. "Are you alright, Gram?" I ask.

"I'm fine, dear. Just struggling with this damn arthritis; it makes it difficult to load the shotgun these days."

I let out a soft chuckle under my breath. "Yeah, Gram I'd imagine that's hell on you. I can load it for you later. I really hate to ask this Gram, but I need you to cancel any reservations you have until everything settles down. I need to keep you and Sarah safe here and that's not possible with strangers constantly comin' and goin' through the front of the house. Since there is always a silver lining, I'll let you know now I'm movin' back in for awhile. I don't want you two here alone."

"No worries, I'm getting too old for all this anyway. I was thinking it might be time to relax and enjoy my great grandbabies."

I snap my head around to look at Gram. "Babies... as in more than one? There is only one stowaway Gram, I saw the ultrasound myself."

"For now, dear." She says over her shoulder as she walks back to her bedroom.

CHAPTER 17

Jake

I sit in my office at the garage, scrolling through hours of security camera footage on my computer screen, feeling frustrated by the lack of progress over the last week. We still have no definitive leads on Michael's location or intentions, and it's driving me crazy. The bastard managed to slip into our small town undetected and has been stalking Sarah relentlessly right under our noses.

Rex enters my office holding two mugs of steaming coffee. He sets one down on my desk and asks, "Any luck finding that psycho fuck on the cameras yet?"

I rub my tired eyes and shake my head. "Nothin' useful so far. I've been searching through footage all over town from the past three days. Lookin' for unfamiliar faces or vehicles that seem out of place. But this is a needle in a damn haystack."

Rex sips his coffee thoughtfully. "We need to change up our strategy here, cuz. Sitting around scoping cameras and waiting for him to screw up again clearly ain't working."

I sigh, knowing he's right. We've been playing defense, reacting to Michael's disturbing threats and attacks. But we need to take control of the situation before he can harm Sarah or the baby.

"So what do you suggest?" I ask Rex. "We're kind of limited in resources here."

Rex sets his mug down, a mischievous smile spreading across his face.

"We bring in the rest of the club, sic Jax on the bastard. Let that genius lil' shit do his hacker voodoo magic. He could probably dig up information on Michael's whereabouts and plans that we would never be able to find the old-fashioned way."

Jackson "Jax" Ford is a member of the Rebel Sons who specializes in computer and tech systems. The kid has impressive hacking skills, capable of breaking into even the most challenging networks. He could be a huge asset.

I nod in agreement. "We should go talk to him and see what information he can gain access to."

After we both finish our coffees, Rex and I hurry to the parking lot where our bikes are parked. In no time, we're speeding down the street towards Riggs Bail and Bounty. The rushing wind helping to clear my thoughts.

As we enter the office, we see Beau hunched over his desk, sorting through piles of paperwork. He looks up and grins at us. "Well, well, if it isn't my two favorite assholes. What brings you boys in?"

"We need Jax's specific skill set," I explained. Beau knows all about the threats against Sarah. "Is he around?"

"I think he's working on a computer in the back room. Let me grab him for you."

A minute later, Jax saunters in with an eager expression on his face. The kid couldn't be any older than early 20's, but he already sported a collection of intricate tattoos that peeked out from under the sleeves of his worn hoodie. Silver gauges in his ears, adding to his rebellious appearance. But don't let his unruly exterior fool you; beneath it lies a brilliant mind.

I give Jax a brief overview of the situation, detailing how Michael Moretti has been stalking Sarah from within our town. However, despite our efforts, we have been unable to track down his whereabouts. "We need you to use your skills and access whatever information you can, specifically a location. Any help in identifying Michael and potential accomplices would be great."

Jax cracks his knuckles, eyes lighting up. "Oh hell yeah, I can totally hack the cameras around town, and traffic cams. If this guy's staying in a hotel or renting a car, I can get into their systems too."

"If you could find out his current location or plans, it would be a game-changer. I have Michael's name, age, and physical description. Any information you can uncover would be incredibly valuable."

"Leave it to me bro," Jax says with a grin. "Just get me set up with my laptop and I'll work my magic. I'll start infiltrating systems and combing through footage until I strike gold. I'm also gonna need about a gallon of energy drinks or my sorcery just isn't as strong."

I clap him on the shoulder, beyond grateful to have his help. "Absolutely man, anything you need. Let me know the second you find anything."

Over the next several hours, Rex and I try to keep busy while Jax works. We catch a bail jumper who missed his court date. I head to the garage to handle some paperwork. But my mind stays hyper-focused on Sarah's safety, hoping Jax can find the break we desperately need.

Close to midnight, my cell phone buzzes with an incoming call from Jax. "Please tell me you have something."

"I got him!" Jax says excitedly. "I found security cam footage of Moretti arriving almost two weeks ago at a rundown motel thirty miles outside of North Ridge. Drove there in a black SUV, looking shady as hell."

Finally, confirmation that the bastard is here. And we have his location. "Text me screen grabs of the footage so I can confirm it's him with Sarah. Great work, Jax."

"Wait, there's more. I hacked the motel's systems and found the room booked under the name Anthony Vitale. I've got his room number now too."

"You're a genius," I tell Jax sincerely. This is the biggest break we've had. "Send all the details. Rex and I are going to pay him a visit."

I quickly call Rex and fill him in on the details, feeling a surge of adrenaline now that we have a solid lead. He agrees to meet me at the motel. I holster my handgun at my waist, hoping it won't be necessary but ready for any scenario. If Michael is backed into a corner, who knows what he might do.

In less than an hour, Rex and I find a spot to park our bikes on the next block over from the rundown motel. At this time of night there isn't a soul in sight on the empty street. Cautiously, we make our way towards Michael's room.

With Rex watching my back, I kick open the flimsy door, gun gripped tightly in my hand. The small space is empty except for a neatly made bed against the wall. My eyes quickly sweep across every inch of the room. And what I see makes my blood turn to ice.

The walls are plastered with photos of Sarah going about her daily routines over the past two weeks. Some are zoomed in shots of her and I around town. Others show her chatting with customers at the Ridge while working. Then my eyes land on a photo of Sarah and me leaving her last prenatal appointment.

The fucker knows. It's not just going to be Sarah he's after now.

Seeing evidence of how closely Michael has been stalking Sarah, right under our noses, fills me with rage. The sick bastard has been studying her every move, preparing for who knows what.

Rex flips on the lights, and we see that Michael has also been surveilling our houses, my garage, the Rigg's Bail & Bounty office. There are pictures of all of us. Proof he's been assessing threats.

I can feel the anger coming from Rex's body the moment he spots a photo of Emmalynn, his four year old daughter, with my sister Cassandra.

Rex's voice is low and dangerous, filled with a seething anger that would make even the toughest men cower. "Brother, if you want your chance at this guy, you better get to him before I do. I'm going to burry this fucker if I get my hands on him." The words drip from his clenched teeth, each syllable laced with venom.

I rub a hand over my mouth, fighting back the bile rising in my throat at the thought of what could have happened if Jax hadn't found Michael's location.

Without wasting any time, Rex gathers Michael's laptop and phone, both valuable sources of information. After wiping surfaces clean of our prints, we clear out before Michael returns.

After returning to Rex's place, Jax wastes no time diving into the task of hacking into the devices. We stand behind him, watching intently as he begins by accessing Michael's phone records.

"Bingo, multiple calls to a burner phone over the last two weeks," Jax announces. "Totally untraceable... well, at least before I do my thing."

It only takes a few minutes for Jax to do his thing. "Got it! The burner phone belongs to Bruno Capparelli, a known criminal involved in operating a chop shop and fencing racket in Portland."

Rex's face darkens. "So Michael's been in contact with Portland criminals since he got to town. We need to figure out what the hell they are up to."

Jax continues digging through Michael's phone and laptop. "There's definitely coordination going on. But all the messages are in code, it's gonna take me some time to decipher all of it."

While Jax keeps searching, I pace anxiously. His surveillance proves Michael has just been biding his time, planning for the right moment to take Sarah. But when?

"There are odd gaps in Michael's history," Jax mutters, brow furrowed in concentration. "His past employment records, education, it's almost like this guy didn't exist before he was 21."

"Can you dig deeper?" Rex asks. "Maybe there's something we could use there."

Jax's fingers fly across the keys. "The gaps look intentional, records scrubbed."

I hover over Jax's shoulder, watching lines of code dance across the screen. My muscles are so tense my neck aches. But finally Jax seems to uncover something sensitive hidden deep in the digital roots of Michael's identity.

"Well I'll be damned," Jax says slowly. "According to data I recovered, Michael Moretti's real name is Anthony Moretti Jr. He's the son of Tony Moretti."

"Moretti..." Rex's eyes widened in disbelief. "Tony Moretti... as in the notorious New Jersey crime boss??"

"Let me make sure I understand correctly. Michael Moretti, who is currently part of the DEA, used to be a member of a prominent crime family?" My mind is having a hard time comprehending this.

Jax nods grimly. "He must have changed his identity to erase all connections to the past. That's why there were gaps. He didn't want background checks tying him to the mob. If it were my guess, I'd say he's still part of the family."

"Jesus," Rex breathes. "That explains how a freaking federal agent could be so violent and deranged. This guy is even more dangerous than we realized."

We're all stunned by this new information on Michael's background. It makes me question what else he's been hiding from Sarah, or involved with that we don't know about.

Jax refocuses on digging through Michael's online activity, searching for anything to explain his plans for Sarah. After attempts to access his cloud accounts and email turn up nothing useful, Jax tries a new angle.

"I'm hacking the burner phone itself now," he explains, fingers flying across the keyboard with precision. "If I can gain access to the network, I may be able to retrieve any deleted text conversations related to their plans."

Rex and I hover anxiously as Jax works, our hopes riding on whatever information he can shake loose. After several tense minutes, his efforts pay off.

"Damn, I'm good." Jax says. "Most texts are coded, but the latest one says the 'package' will be delivered tomorrow night at 11pm...I think he means Sarah."

"We need to grab Sarah now and get her on the compound," Rex says urgently, already gathering weapons and gear.

As Jax's eyes remain glued to the screen, "Guys... We need to get Cassandra and Emmalynn secured too. From the information I have found so far, the Moretti's are running a trafficking operation in California, using girls as payment to the cartel in exchange for smuggling drugs across the Mexican border back into Cali."

Rex's face turns pale as he mutters to himself, "The pictures of Emmalynn and Cassandra at the park... the pictures of them he had hanging in the motel room."

My heart pounds with adrenaline and rage. "Let's go get the girls secured," I tell Rex grimly. "Then we hunt this mother fucker down and finish him."

CHAPTER 18

Sarah

I sit at the worn kitchen table across from Marlene, clutching a warm mug of coffee between my hands. The rising sun filters in through lace curtains, casting a soft glow across Marlene's kind face. She smiles gently at me from over the rim of her own coffee cup, the faint crow's feet at the corners of her eyes crinkling.

"More coffee, dear?" Marlene asks, gesturing at my nearly empty mug. I nod and slide it towards her.

As Marlene stands to grab the coffee pot, my cell phone on the table suddenly buzzes to life, vibrating loudly against the wood. I glance at the caller ID flashing across the screen and see that it's Jake. Swiping to answer, I lift the phone to my ear.

"Hello?"

"Hey baby, it's me," Jake's low voice rumbles through the speaker.

"Hey Jake, what's up?" I ask casually, hoping my inner fluster at the sound of his voice isn't detectable through the phone.

"Listen, we've got plans in motion to get you, Cassandra, Gram, and Emmalynn moved somewhere safe. I'm on my way now to come pick you and Gram up from the B&B. Rex is headed to grab Emmalynn and Cassandra from his place and we'll all meet back at the B&B. Some of my guys from the club are gonna provide escort on their bikes and make sure we get to the compound without trouble."

Jake's words spill out in a rush and I grip the phone tighter, processing what he's saying. I let out a breath, feeling relieved that we've got a strategy in place. As long as we can make it to the compound, Michael won't be able to get to me, or hurt anyone else trying. The likelihood that he'll expect me to seek refuge with an outlaw motorcycle club is low.

"Okay. That sounds good," I tell Jake.

"Pack a bag with anything important you wanna take. We may be there a while. I'll see you soon, Darlin'. Miss you."

"Miss you," I echo, and with that, the call ends. I set my phone down on the table as Marlene returns with a steaming pot of coffee.

"What was that all about?" she asks curiously, refilling my mug.

"That was Jake. He's on his way to come get us. Him and Rex have a plan to get all of us safely to the club compound, away from Michael."

Marlene's expression turns serious and she nods. "Well then, we best get to packing up our bags as quickly as we can."

We quickly finish our coffee and then make our way upstairs. In my small bedroom, I grab the worn backpack I arrived with and begin neatly packing away some clothes, toiletries, and other essentials. I don't have much, so it doesn't take long. As I'm zipping up the bag, a loud bang suddenly echoes from downstairs, making me jump.

My heart starts hammering in my chest as I stand frozen. What was that sound? I crack open my bedroom door and peek out into the hallway, listening intently. I can hear the distinct sounds of someone moving around on the lower level of the house.

Panic grips me then as I realize someone must have broken into Marlene's house. It has to be Michael. He must have been waiting and watching the place, saw his chance and took it.

As quietly as I can, I close my door again. I've got to find somewhere to hide, and quickly. I squeeze myself into the back of the closet, pulling the doors shut as I try to control my panicked breathing. In a rush, I pull my phone out and silence the ringer.

Heavy boots stomp up the stairs, the floorboards creaking under their weight. They stride purposefully towards my room and then the door is thrown violently open, banging against the wall. My whole body trembles. Through the crack in the closet doors, I see Michael stalk into view, head swiveling left and right as he searches for me. My blood turns to ice. It's taking everything in me not to make a sound as I watch him.

After a few agonizing minutes of him rifling through the room, he curses loudly and storms back out without finding me. I let out a sigh of relief.

I stay frozen for a minute longer, listening. I can still hear Michael banging around angrily downstairs. Steeling my nerves, I slowly emerge from the closet and tiptoe toward the door. I pause there, listening again for any sounds of movement.

Hearing nothing close by, I carefully sneak out into the hall and make my way toward the stairs. I have no idea where Marlene is in the house, or if she's okay. I just need to get outside. Jake will be here any minute.

As I reach the top of the stairs, an ear splitting blast echoes through the house, the unmistakable boom of a shotgun being fired. I scream in shock before quickly clamping my hand over my mouth.

"You get the hell out of my house, you no good bastard! I'm shootin' your dick off with the next one!" Marlene's voice rings out fiercely. Oh my god, that was her shotgun!

I hear Michael swearing up a storm followed by the sound of the back door slamming shut. Marlene must have scared him off with the shotgun. Thank god she's okay.

Not wasting another second, I bolt down the stairs and race for the front door. I burst outside into the cool morning air, heart pounding wildly. Frantically I look around expecting to see Michael still nearby.

Just then, I hear the roar of Jake's motorcycle engine. I turn to see him speeding up the gravel driveway towards me, his face etched with concern.

I wave my arms to get his attention, running toward him. "Jake!" I yell.

He pulls to a stop beside me, gravel skittering under his back tire. His handsome face is etched with concern.

"Michael broke in," I rush to explain without preamble. "I think Marlene might've scared him off with her shotgun. I heard it go off." I rush out breathlessly.

Jake's expression darkens with fury. We both turn at the sound of an engine revving from behind the B&B. A second later, Michael's black SUV peels out from the back driveway, fishtailing onto the road as he speeds away.

With a scowl, Jake kicks his bike back into gear. "Get inside and make sure Gram is okay. I'm going after the son of a bitch."

Before I can respond, Jake takes off after Michael in a spray of gravel, his bike quickly disappearing from view.

My heart pounds, both from adrenaline and fear for Jake. Pushing down my anxiety, I rush back inside to check on Marlene. I find her in the kitchen, hastily shoving shotgun shells into her apron pocket.

"Marlene! Are you okay?" I ask frantically, scanning her for injuries.

"I'm fine, I'm fine," as she waves my concern away, clearly still amped up on adrenaline.

"That coward broke in the back door but scurried off quick once I let loose with Betsy here." She hefts the shotgun in demonstration.

I let out a tense breath. "Thank god you're alright. And that you had Betsy handy," I say with a shaky laugh. Marlene just gives a satisfied smirk in response.

We peer out the window toward the driveway but there's no sign of Jake or Michael yet. I anxiously drum my fingers on the counter, trying to ignore the twist of fear in my gut. Jake can handle himself, I know he can. Still, I'll feel a lot better once I see him riding back up that driveway in one piece.

Marlene seems to read my mind. "Don't you worry about our boy," she says, giving my arm a pat. "Jake's too stubborn to let the likes of that sorry bastard get the better of him."

I nod, hoping she's right. Jake has always been a survivor. Even as a broken, troubled youth, he had an inner strength. A will to endure, no matter what life threw at him.

We pass the time waiting for Jake's return by having another cup of coffee and triple checking we have everything packed and ready to go. My nerves feel frayed, but having Marlene's steady presence keeps me from unraveling completely.

CHAPTER 19

Jake

I drive my bike up the gravel driveway of the B&B, scanning the surroundings for any sign of trouble. Sarah's face is filled with fear as she runs towards me from the front porch. As I skid to a stop beside her, the screeching sound of tires draws my attention. Michael's black SUV comes fishtailing down the driveway behind the house, kicking up gravel as he speeds toward the main road.

Fuming, I kick my bike back into gear and take off after him, determined not to let the fucker get away. I dart onto the main road, skillfully navigating through the quiet streets in town as I chase after him. In the distance, Michael's SUV swerves erratically between lanes, obviously attempting to shake me off his tail. But I'm not going to let that happen. I push my bike harder, not letting the SUV out of my sight.

We're almost out of town when Michael makes a sharp turn onto a dirt road leading into thick forest. I stay glued to his bumper as dust plumes up behind the SUV. Determined not to lose sight of his vehicle as dust rises up in clouds around me. The trees blur past me, but I hold on tight to my handlebars, my focus solely on keeping up with him. He doesn't have much further to go; the dumbass drove onto a dead-end road.

After about a mile, he slams on the brakes and comes to a sudden stop, sending another cloud of dust into the air. I skidded to a halt behind him, gravel flying from beneath my tires. In one swift movement, I kill the engine and leap off the bike, ready to deliver the just retribution this mother fucker has coming to him.

Michael throws open the driver's side door, pointing a handgun directly at me. My body tenses in response. "Give it up. You've got nowhere else to run," I caution, standing my ground. Anger takes over Michael's face as he rushes towards me, firing off two haphazard shots in rapid succession. I quickly drop to the ground and roll, narrowly escaping the bullets. As soon as I regain my footing, I charge at him. Throwing him to the ground with so much force his head bounces off the road in a deafening thud.

We exchange blows as we wrestle for control of the weapon still gripped in his hand. I drive my elbow viciously into his face, momentarily dazing him. Taking advantage of the opportunity, I grip his wrist and slam it repeatedly against a nearby rock in the road. He cries out in pain and finally drops the gun. Now that I have him disarmed, I unleash all the rage coursing through me in a whirlwind of punches to Michael's face and body. I hold nothing back.

The memory of each tear rolling down Sarah's face as she shared the details of the abuse at this fuckers hands, fuels each punch I deliver. Michael struggles weakly to defend himself. Without his gun, he's no match for my strength and extensive combat training from my time in the Marines. His face is now bloodied, and his eyes glazed. He tries to crawl away from me, but I grab him by the hair and pull him back up to look me in the eye.

"Did you let her go when it was too much for her to bear? Did you let her escape and run away when she pleaded for you to stop? When she begged for your mercy?" Not waiting for a reply, "No, you didn't, and you sure as fuck won't be gettin' any mercy from me."

With all my force, I drive my knee up into his stomach. He doubles over in pain, wheezing for air, unable to fight back as I continue my relentless attack. Through gritted teeth I growl, "You'll never lay a hand on her again, motherfucker!"

I'm only vaguely aware of the sound of an approaching engine over the rage clouding my mind. "Jake!" The sound of Beau's voice breaks through my mental fog, and I turn my head to look at him. Michael takes the opportunity in my brief moment of distraction to reach for a knife he had hidden. My eyes are drawn to the glint of metal in Michael's hand as he sinks the blade of the knife deep into my shoulder, just below my clavicle.

My body is too flooded with adrenaline, to feel any pain. With a swift motion, I remove the knife and forcefully plunge it into Michael's chest.

Fighting for air, he manages to choke out, "In her mind, she'll always be my broken and used whore. She will never escape me." As the blood pools around his motionless body, his breaths become shallow and soon cease altogether.

"Jesus Christ," Beau curses under his breath. "You know this is the beginning of a war, right? Tony Moretti is going to come after you and the club with everything he's got."

"Let him fucking come," I roar. "That bastard deserved what he got, and then some. I'll take on anyone that dares to come our way. He can send an entire goddamn army and it won't make a difference. I'll do whatever it takes. Slaughter every one of his men, one by fucking one, to keep Sarah, our family, and my club safe."

"Son, I understand, and I'll be right there with you, side by side. We gotta be prepared, this will be one hell of a fight. Let's head back to the B&B. Rex is there waiting on us, watching over the women. For now, I still want them to stay at the compound. Let's get them taken care of, then I'll call church and fill the rest of the boys in on what went down. I'll send the prospects to clean this shit up. Grab the knife, just in case someone comes across the body before it gets dealt with."

As my anger dissipates, I start to feel the physical toll of my actions. My knuckles and shoulder throb in pain, and I can feel bruises and scrapes on my body. But at this moment, my own injuries are the least of my concerns. My main focus is getting back to Sarah.

CHAPTER 20

Sarah

My nerves are on edge as we wait for Jake to return. He had taken off in pursuit of Michael and none of us knew when, or if he would come back. Suddenly, the distant rumble of engines catches my attention, and I run out the front door. I hurry down the steps toward the driveway, scanning desperately for that first glimpse of Jake so I can breathe again knowing he's OK. Finally, they appear in the distance, kicking up dust as they race towards us. Jake and Beau side by side.

Jake looks every inch the fearsome warrior and I drink in the sight of him. His large muscular frame sitting astride his bike. His strong, tattooed arms tightly gripping the handlebars. His handsome face is set in a determined expression accentuated by the dark stubble covering his jaw. Relief floods me simply seeing him whole and alive before me.

As he comes closer, my eyes widen in shock at the sight of blood drenching his black t-shirt and splattered across his neck and hands. The bile rises in my throat as I take in the dark stain starting at his shoulder, spreading down the entire left side of his body. Panic sets in as Jake comes to a stop next to me, but all I can focus on is the vivid red dripping down the polished chrome of his bike.

I can't believe what I'm seeing. "Jake, are you okay?" My voice trembles, and I instinctively reach out to him, but then pull back unsure if my touch would cause more pain. Jake gently takes my trembling hand in his rough, calloused ones for comfort.

"Just a flesh wound, baby. Nothing to worry that pretty head about." His deep voice holds a nonchalant tone, but I can't tear my eyes from the wound I now notice marring the smooth, tanned skin just below his collarbone. The ragged incision oozes a steady flow of dark blood down Jake's chest and side despite his dismissive words.

I feel myself starting to lose control and panic, but Jake's deep voice snaps me back to reality. "Look at me, Darlin'. Take a deep breath," he says in his gruff tone. I gather my composure with determination and lock eyes with him, nodding quickly. "I'm fine, you're fine, we're all fine, baby," he reassures me. "You need to stay calm; it's not good for the baby if you're upset and stressed."

The front door creaks open, then clicks shut. Over my shoulder, Jake shouts for his sister Cassandra to fetch the first aid kit and a couple of towels.

Beau is straddling his Harley, parked next to Jake's bike, finishing up a phone call where he is barking orders at prospects. He then stomps over to my side, his chiseled face mirroring the worry and unease that I feel inside.

Cassandra and Rex emerge from the house in a hurry, carrying a first aid kit, towels, and bottles of water. Jake carefully removes his shirt and tosses it aside. He reaches for the kit from Cassandra's grasp, but she pulls it back.

"For the past three years, you've been paying for my nursing school tuition. So maybe, just for a few minutes, you could put aside your pride and macho bullshit, and let me help you for a change. After all, you should at least get your damn money's worth out of me."

Jake's lips curl into a small smirk as he nods slightly, giving Cassandra the go-ahead.

Rex voiced the question that was on all of our minds. "So you got the fucker?"

"He's no longer a concern for any of us." Jake replied, his eyes locked with mine.

Feeling unsure about Jake's statement, I asked, "I'm not sure what that means, Jake."

"It means you don't have to worry about that bastard ever again. He won't come searching for you or our child." The firm tone in Jake's voice tells me not to ask for further explanation, and I doubt I would receive one even if I did.

As Cassandra finishes up cleaning and dressing Jake's wound using a basic first aid kit, the distinct sound of motorcycles catches our attention. Two riders, both wearing the Rebel Sons' emblem on their kuttes, pull up the driveway, parking behind Jake and Beau. Jake squeezes my shoulders in a reassuring manner.

"It's alright, just some of my brothers." He waves the leather-clad men over. "Darlin', this here's Xavier Grant, everyone calls him X, and Talon Vaugn. Boys, this is Sarah, my old lady."

Both men acknowledge my presence with a polite nod. Talon is the first to greet me with a tight handshake, and I return the gesture. X, on the other hand, walks around Jake's bike to where I'm standing and surprises me by pulling me into a giant bearhug. His massive build completely envelops my body in a tight, borderline inappropriate, embrace.

"Make sure to get my number from Jake. You ever decide to trade up, give me a call sweetheart."

Jake steps closer and pulls me back to him. "You'll have to excuse my brother, baby. He's a bit of a man whore and really wants his ass kicked today."

I try to hide my amusement at X's obvious attempt to piss off Jake.

X is tall and lean, but incredibly muscular. Colorful tattoos cover his arms and neck. His dark hair is styled in a messy, yet intentional, way and his piercing green eyes seem to hold a glint of mischief. According to his patch he is the club's Sergeant at Arms.

Talon stands with an air of confidence, his kutte proudly displaying the Road Captain patch. I can't see any tattoos on his arms or neck. His dark hair is slicked back in a traditional style and his jawline is defined by a perfectly groomed beard. He could easily trade in his kutte for a business suit, and you wouldn't even question it.

"Come on boys, time to stop fucking off and get shit done. Our main priority is getting the women safely inside our compound as soon as possible." Beau yells while mounting his bike.

Our bags are already loaded in the back of Rex's truck. Marlene gets into the front, while Cassandra, Emmalynn, and I get into the back. As Rex puts the truck into gear, Beau and Jake pull their bikes in front of the truck. X and Talon riding behind us.

Over the sound of all the engines, I hear Beau shouting orders to the men on the bikes.

"Let's keep it tight and keep your heads on swivel. Anything pops off, we ride hard and fast, create distance. Understood?"

"Understood, Prez," X responded, his voice gravelly but clear. Talon simply revved his engine in agreement, the rumble a growl of readiness.

"Alright, stay vigilant, let's roll out!" Jake yells.

About 10 minutes after leaving the B&B, we turn off the main road onto a paved private drive. The drive is long, about a mile, trees lining both sides. As we approach the gates of the Rebel Sons compound, my eyes widen at the sight of the security measures in place. Tall fences, cameras, and armed guards give the place an air of fortress-like security. Rex navigates through the entrance, and I can't help but feel a mix of relief and apprehension.

Once inside it looks more like a ranch. Rex starts explaining to me the layout of the compound as we drive through. " The drive splits off in three ways. Turn left and we have the garages. The smaller garage bays over there," Rex pointed, his finger tracing the line of large, open doors where bikes and cars gleamed under the fluorescent glow. "Maintenance and upgrades, all handled by the brothers. We take pride in our wheels. The larger garage holds our fleet of semis used for our transport business.

The drive leading straight ahead goes to the main club house." The main clubhouse is massive and absolutely beautiful. Not what one would expect to find pulling up to a biker clubhouse. The log cabin building stands tall and proud, its wooden walls contrasting against the sturdy and rustic stone foundation. The stones are a mix of warm browns, grays, and creams, creating a natural and inviting feeling.

"The drive to the right, where we are going, leads to a row of 10 townhouses, one for each of the 7 members that hold officer positions. We keep three vacant units for visiting chapter presidents. That drive then goes around to the back of the club house where there is a two-story building that houses 1-bedroom apartments for any members who want to live on the compound. It also has one larger communal space with bunks for any visiting members."

We arrive at the row of townhouses, each one a miniature version of the main clubhouse made to look like a log cabin. Each unit has a mailbox placed beside its front door, clearly labeled indicating which club officer the townhouse is designated for.

"Safe and sound, Sarah," Rex assured me, his voice steady as the truck rolled to a stop. "Welcome home."

I glanced around, taking in the sight of the homes reserved for the club's officers and their families. Before I realized it Jake was beside the truck opening the door for me.

"Come on, baby. Let's Grab your bag and get you inside." Jake reaches for my hand to help me out of the truck.

"Alright, ladies and gentlemen," Beau's voice cut through the air, raw and commanding. He was already off his bike, his posture tense with authority. "Church in 20 minutes. Get your shit together."

I watched him stalk away, boots thudding against the paved drive, a man on a mission with no time for hesitation or delay. His urgency driving home the gravity of what had transpired, and what was yet to come.

"Church?" I asked.

"Club meeting," Jake explained, his gray eyes scanning the area with an intensity that told me he was always on alert. "We'll discuss... business."

"Business," I echoed.

"Sarah," Jake said, his voice a low purr that sent a shiver down my spine. "You're with me now. Remember that. I won't always be able to tell you everything. That's to protect you just as much as the club. You just gotta trust I'll always do right by you, even if I can't tell you what I'm doin'."

I nod in agreement then move around to the back of the truck to grab my bag. I follow Jake to his townhouse. Cassandra starts to come with us when Jake stops her.

"Cass, I'm fine, it ain't deep," he insists gruffly. "I need to talk to Sarah alone for a minute."

"You need to get that wound stitched up, Jake. Don't come crying to me when it gets infected." She heads towards Rex's townhouse as she speaks.

Jake holds the door open, and I walk inside. Muted light filters through the windows illuminating rustic leather furniture and a giant wooden dining table.

"I wasn't completely truthful back there at the B&B. Figured Beau and I should fill everyone in together about what really went down." He scrubs one large, calloused hand across the harsh scruff covering his jaw. The tension radiating off Jake amps higher by the second putting my nerves on high alert.

"Truth is, I killed Michael. Stabbed him after he pulled a knife and stabbed me. That's not what I need to talk to you about though. I know this ain't gonna be easy to hear. But you deserve to know the bastard's full truth." Jake's jaw clenches, fury brewing in his flinty gaze.

"Far as we can tell, Michael ain't just a fed. He's a high level boss workin' for the Moretti crime family out East. Been running drugs, illegal weapons, maybe even..." He pauses, dragging a hand roughly down his face. "Our intel says he also oversees the family's human trafficking ring on the west coast."

"No!" I gasp out a choked sob. "I swear Jake, I didn't know about any of this! I just wanted to get away from the abuse and keep my baby safe."

"Shh, I know. I know you didn't, baby," he rumbles softly. "I just wanted you to hear this from me. You deserved to hear the truth from me, to know before all my brothers do. I gotta go to church, figure out our next moves." Jake brushes gentle knuckles over my wet cheek. "You gonna be okay alone for a bit?"

I nod weakly. Shooting me one last concerned glance, Jake stalks out the door, fury radiating from his powerful frame with each long-legged stride.

Alone with my thoughts, I wonder how many women Michael has hurt. I thought it was only Anna and me. I can hardly comprehend the truths I've learned today. Moving to the bathroom on shaky legs, I rinse the tear tracks from my swollen face.

Exhaustion takes over as I eye Jake's bed. Unable to resist the comfort it represents, I curl atop the quilted blankets. Breathing deep, I let Jake's scent envelop me, imagining the safety of his strong arms. My eyes drift closed, emotionally and physically spent. I fall asleep knowing Michael is dead and he can never get to my child.

CHAPTER 21

Jake

I enter the clubhouse through the heavy wooden doors, which close with a dull thud behind me. Ahead of me is the spacious common room which is empty right now. To my left is the President's office and to my right is the entrance to the chapel, reserved only for patched members of the Rebel Sons. This space serves as a meeting room for handling all club affairs.

Making my way into the chapel, I head towards the long wooden rectangular table. The club's emblem of a winged skull is carved in the center, serving as a reminder of our brotherhood. As I approach, I can feel their eyes follow me, taking in my disheveled and bloodied state. They must have questions, but they will wait until church begins before speaking out of turn.

I give a quick nod of acknowledgment as I walk towards my usual spot on the right side of the President. The Vice President, Rex, always takes the seat to the President's left. Moving down the table to Rex's left is X, our trusted Sergeant at Arms, followed by Jett, who serves as our club Secretary. To my right sits Talon, our Road Captain, and then Gunnar, who handles all financial matters as our Treasurer.

The remaining spots at the table are filled by our members who don't hold an officer position in the club. Pop and Ox are two of the original founding members of the Rebel Sons, with Pops being Gunnar's father.

My little brother Wyatt patched in about a year ago. Then there is Jax our resident tech geek, expert in all things tech and hacking. And finally, there's Patch, our club doctor who is standing beside my seat waiting for me, his medical bag and supplies ready.

I tilt my head away from him, giving him room to get to work on the stab wound. Patch takes an alcohol-soaked cloth and presses it against the rough, jagged cut. I wince at the sharp sting, unable to hold back my reaction.

"Sorry, brother," Patch mutters as he cleans the wound. His brows are furrowed in concentration as he works. Once finished, he pulls out a needle and thread and begins stitching the wound closed with practiced precision. I remain stoic, refusing to show any more outward signs of pain.

After what seems an eternity, Patch ties off the final stitch and covers the area with a clean bandage. I clap him on the back in thanks before grabbing a clean shirt and pulling it over my head. Patch gathers his supplies and takes his seat as I settle into mine.

Heavy boots thud loudly against the hardwood floor as Beau enters the chapel with a determined stride, my uncle's imposing figure emanating strength. As president of this chapter and the mother chapter at that, his mere presence demands respect. He moves towards the head of the table with a rigid posture, jaw set, and eyes flashing with intensity. With a forceful motion, Beau slams his fist down onto the surface, the sound reverberating through the room.

"Church is now in session," he announces. "Lock it up."

The men turn their attention to our President, a respectful silence settling over the room.

"I'll keep this brief." Beau's voice is a low rumble as he surveys the room. "Jake and I had a... situation... with an DEA agent earlier.

Michael Moretti."

I interject to provide more information, as Beau rests his hands on the table, visibly tense. I recount arriving at the B&B and finding Michael fleeing after a failed attempt at kidnapping Sarah. Chasing after him, and the tense altercation that turned violent. And my eventual act of self-defense when Michael pulled a knife and stabbed me. My brothers listen intently, their stern gazes showing no judgment or doubt.

"This Michael Moretti..." I hesitate, glancing toward Beau for the go ahead before continuing. At his subtle nod I push forward, knowing I have to claim Sarah and the baby in front of my brothers. Then they will both be under the protection of the club.

"He was Sarah's husband. She ran from him to protect herself, and the baby she's carrying. My woman, my baby. I'm claiming them both now in front of the club." At that I look around the room at all my brothers, gauging their reaction.

"He beat her the entire time they were married. It wasn't just a slap here or there; she has scars all over her body from lashings. I guess the fucker liked using a leather belt on her. She's had broken bones on multiple occasions. It was so bad a few times he almost killed her. It went beyond the physical abuse. Sarah was sexual assaulted too. She hasn't gone into too much detail about that with me. From what she has told me, it was damn near a daily occurrence over the 12 years she was married to the bastard.

He's not just a DEA agent; he's also the son of Tony Moretti, the boss of the Moretti Crime Family on the east coast. According to what Jax has been able to uncover so far, the old man handles business out east while Michael takes care of matters on the west coast. However, his father does travel west. Jax has been watching his movements and he appears to fly out a few times a month. Their main operation out west is a trafficking ring that sends girls to Mexico as payment for drugs being brought into the country by the cartel for the Moretti's to distribute."

A heavy silence fills the room. The weight of the revelation hangs heavily in the air as my brothers, and I process the gravity of our current situation. A threat that I brought to my brother's doorsteps.

The club and my brothers are all strong believers in treating women with respect. None of my brothers will tolerate any kind of abuse towards women. Their silent anger is palpable as they learn about the abuse my old lady lived through. At the thought of what all the other women they are trafficking must be going through right now.

My younger brother, Wyatt, breaks the silence. "Jake, you should have brought this to the table earlier. We're here for you and Sarah. She's my sister now, and she's carrying my soon-to-be niece or nephew. Whatever you need, just say the word."

Gunnar speaks up next, sharing his thoughts. "Once you claimed her, Sarah became a sister to all of us. That child is a new niece or nephew to us all. Not just Wyatt, we're all in this together. If they want a war, we'll give them one. We are brothers until the end. We ride together, we rise together, we die together. Sons forever."

Every man seated around the table nods in unison and chants, "We ride together, we rise together, we die together. Sons forever."

"Thank you," with gratitude, I address my brothers at the table. Trying to hide the emotions churning inside me as they openly accept my decision to raise Sarah's child as my own.

"While I appreciate all the support for Sarah, we have more than just Sarah to protect." I turn my gaze to Rex, silently asking if he wants to be the one to share this information. He nods for me to continue. "Jax found the intel on where Moretti was staying locally. Rex and I searched his motel room. We came across several photos of Emmalynn and Cassandra together in various locations. Some were taken at the park, Cass taking Emmalynn out for ice cream, and entering and exiting Rex's house. It was clear someone had been watching them closely. We now realize after the intel Jax has uncovered so far; they are targets of the trafficking ring being run by the Moretti organization. Likely as a way to retaliate against me, and likely our club, for protecting Sarah."

Beau flies up from his seat, causing his chair to collide with the wall behind him as his anger boils over.

"Any motherfucker who dares to lay a finger on my granddaughter will meet their fucking maker by my hands!"

"No way in hell will anyone ever get to Cass. I'll kill every sorry bastard they send who is fool enough to try. As long as I'm breathing, Cass will never be a salve to any man."

X's unexpected outburst over my sister catches me and everyone else off guard, but that's a discussion for a later time. There are far more urgent matters that need my attention.

As we're discussing the possibility of retaliation from the Moretti family, Beau's phone starts ringing. The sound breaking through the tense air of the room. Beau answers on speakerphone, and I immediately recognize Dom's voice. Dom is one of the club's prospects that was given the task of cleaning up the mess I left behind.

"Prez, I'm at the location. There's no sign of Moretti or his vehicle, just the pool of blood on the gravel like you mentioned. Wanted to double check that this is the right spot before we continued searching. You said Raiders Ridge Road, right? Where the road dead ends?"

"Yeah boy, that's the spot," Beau confirms gruffly then ends the call. Beau's jaw tightens, the muscles in his neck cording with tension.

"Son of a bitch," Rex curses under his breath. "He must have had a crew with him we didn't see around town, and a tracker on the SUV. They grabbed the body before our guys got there."

I scrub a hand down my face, the day's events catching up with me. "Or it means I fucked up and the bastard is still breathing. We gotta assume he's still alive until we have confirmation. I regret not putting a bullet between the fucker's eyes. I didn't want to leave evidence behind on a federal agent that could be linked back to me or the club. But I watched him stop breathing."

Beau nods grimly and says, "You made the right call, Jake." Then he turns to Jax. "Keep an eye on Moretti, and the old man's movements. If there's any talk within the organization about Michael's whereabouts, I want to be informed right away."

Jax nods and begins scribbling down notes, always eager to showcase his abilities and prove himself an asset to the club. The kid's got skills when it comes to gathering intel and hacking. If there's any digital footprint or communication about Michael, Jax will find it.

Beau addresses the group once more, determination etched into his rugged features. "This threat from the Moretti's changes nothing. The 40th anniversary celebration on the Fourth goes on as planned. I will not let that arrogant prick derail or overshadow a celebration forty years in the making." He slams a fist down for emphasis. "My father founded this club, carved this empire out of nothing but dust and grit. And we will honor that legacy as intended in two weeks time. Understood?"

Murmurs of assent sound from the men around the table. Pride swells in my chest for the reaper we all wear. For the family and brotherhood forged here. For the empire my grandfather built from the ground up, and for my uncle continuing the vision of his father, my grandfather, that we all now protect. This club runs through my veins as sure as blood. It gave me purpose when I had none. Became the family I never had growing up. I'll be damned if I let the Moretti's take that from us.

Beau then hands out orders for the week. "Jett, Gunnar, Ox, and Talon, you're all on transport. All the paperwork is on the clipboard in the office. Take care of it. Rex and Wyatt, we got a skip to track down. The guy is out on an assault charge. You boys are on your own on this one. I want all of Jax's focus on the Moretti situation, and Jake has the garage to manage.

Jake, the prospects, X, and I will help you in the garage this week and with keeping an eye on the girls when they leave the compound. If Em, Cass, or Sarah step foot outside of these gates, a member or prospect is with them, or has eyes on them at all times.

You all have your jobs to do, get out of here and handle your shit. Jake, you hang back, I want to speak with you privately for a minute."

One by one, my brothers all exit the chapel, leaving just Beau and I sitting at the table. He places a hand on my shoulder, a look of pride mixed with concern in his eyes.

"You handled yourself well today in an impossible situation. Protected the club, protected your family. I'm proud of you nephew, never doubt that."

I swallow down the sudden thickness in my throat and nod, unable to find words for the praise I crave yet so rarely receive from this gruff, man who stepped up as the only father figure I've ever known.

After another weighted moment, Beau drops his hand and stands abruptly. "Go on and check on your old lady now. Make sure she's settled in alright after the day she's had."

I don't need to be told twice. In no time I'm striding up the paved drive toward the row of townhouses reserved for club officers. I find her curled up asleep in my bed looking so damn beautiful and peaceful. Can't resist brushing a strand of hair back from her face.

Realizing I'm grimy and blood spattered still, I strip and grab a quick shower. The hot water sluicing over my skin takes some tension with it down the drain. Toweling off briskly, I pull on boxers and a clean t-shirt. Sarah stirs at the dip of the mattress as I slide in next to her, wrapping my body protectively around hers.

"Shh, just sleep baby," I murmur against her hair as she burrows back into my warmth.

Sometime later she stirs restlessly in my arms. I rub her back, murmuring soothing words until she stills again. I know Sarah's got a lot to process with everything that's happened. Learning the ugly truths about who Michael Moretti really was and the danger he still poses. She's been through hell, but I aim to give her the safety and love she deserves now.

As if on cue, Sarah's stomach lets out a loud rumble and I realize neither of us have eaten anything since yesterday. Idiot that I am, I didn't even think to get her food despite knowing she's eating for two now.

"Let's grab some dinner, Darlin'," I suggest, pulling her up gently with me.

We make our way to the clubhouse and head straight to the kitchen, following our noses to whatever savory concoction Gram has simmering on the stove. Sarah inhales deeply, the hint of a smile finally touching her lips.

Gram looks up from her cooking, beaming brightly when she sees Sarah.

"There you are, sweetie! Sit down now and let me get you a plate. Gotta feed my great grand baby."

Sarah does as she's told, digging into the tender pot roast, roasted veggies and buttery mashed potatoes Gram slides in front of her. I fix my own overflowing plate and take a seat beside her at the table.

As Sarah eats, I give her the rundown on Gram.

"Gram here was the first old lady of this club, you know," I explain for Sarah's benefit. "Married my grandfather, one of the founding members and the first President. She's the backbone that held this place together back in the early days. Stood by Gramps' side as he built the club into what it is today. She has always been the nurturing matriarch of the Rebel Sons, making sure her boys are fed and cared for. All the brothers love when she visits." Sarah listens intently as she eats.

Once finished, I offer to give Sarah a full tour of the compound so she can get familiar with the place that's now her home for the time being. I show her the garages, and the apartments for members behind the clubhouse. Between the back of the clubhouse and the apartments there is an outdoor area with a firepit and built in benches around it. A play area for the kids of members. An outdoor kitchen with multiple grills. A stone patio with rows of picnic tables. I take her through the entire sprawling compound, watching as she focuses intently on each aspect, committing it to memory.

Exhaustion evident on her lovely face, I suggest turning in early tonight. Sarah readily agrees and we make our way back to my townhouse hand in hand.

In bed, I curl myself around her once more, splaying one large hand over her stomach. I'm not expecting it when I feel a sudden strong push against my palm. Sarah's sharp intake of breath tells me she felt it too. Our eyes meet, wide with awe.

"Was that the baby?"

"Sure was, and we both got to feel the baby move for the first time together." The emotion was thick in Sarah's voice.

As we settle in, Sarah reminds me about her ultrasound

appointment tomorrow after her shift at the Ridge. This is the appointment we will find out the sex of the baby.

I curse internally, hating that I'd forgotten something so important. "I wouldn't miss it for the world, baby," I assure her. Already planning to have Rex drive us into town in the morning so I can get my truck from the garage. No way in hell I'm taking Sarah on my bike in her condition. Her and our little one's safety is my top priority now. With Sarah wrapped securely in my arms, I let the comfort of her soft breaths lull me to sleep.

CHAPTER 22

Sarah

On my break at the Ridge, I type a quick text to Jake. Hoping he isn't too deep into a build or some engine that he doesn't see the text.

> *Me: Hey, any chance you could pick me up a little early today? Sophia wants to talk to us about something, around 3:00. Seemed important.*

> *Jake: Us as in me and you? What would she need to talk to us about?*

> *Me: I'm not sure, she didn't give me any details. She just asked if we could talk to her today. She also wanted Beau and Rex to come if they had time.*

Jake: Yeah, baby. I'll make it work. Beau is with me today, he said he'd be there. He's calling Rex now to see if he can swing by. Love you

Me: Love you too, miss you and your ass :)

Jake: My ass misses you too Darlin', but not as much as my dick. He's damn near cryin'. See you at 3:00, behave.

I slide my phone back into the pocket of my apron and head back out to the bar. I try to concentrate on working, but my mind keeps wandering. I'm worried about Sophia and what she might need to speak with us about.

Right at 3:00 I see Jake's truck pull up in front of the Ridge. He's followed by Beau and Rex. All three men walk through the front door and head towards me. I walk out from behind the bar and Jake gives me a hug and a quick kiss.

"You know what this is about?" Beau directs his question at me.

"No Beau, I don't. She didn't tell me anything except she would like to talk with all of us. Sophia is in her office waiting on us."

All four of us walk back into the hallway past the restrooms to the far end of the hall where Sophia's office is. I knock on the door and Sophia calls out for me to come in.

"Hey Sophia, the guys are here."

"Good, come in. I only have two chairs but two of you can sit on the sofa."

Beau and Rex take the chairs in front of Sophia's desk. Jake sits on the couch, I move to sit beside him but he grabs me by the waist and pulls me down on his lap. One arm wrapped around my back, his hand resting on my belly. The other arm is across my legs with his fingers stroking up and down my outer thigh.

"Thank you for coming," Sophia began, her voice wavering. "I know you guys are all busy, but there's something important I need to share." She hesitated, taking a deep breath to steady herself before continuing.

"When I was 11, I was taken a few blocks from my home when I was walking home from a friend's house." Her voice broke on the word 'taken,' tears pooling in her eyes.

Jake's hand found mine, his strong grip both comforting and grounding. I could feel the tension radiating from him as we hang on Sophia's every word.

"I was terrified, alone. They brought me to a house where I was kept with other girls. Some of the girls were younger, most were older than I was."

Sophia paused, old anguish and pain etched on her face. She seemed to retreat into her memories for a moment before visibly gathering her resolve.

"All of the girls were eventually sent away. From what I over heard during my time there, they were first sent to a warehouse. It was somewhere on the west coast. I heard the men talking about a dock and shipping containers. They were then sent to Mexico. But Tony... he kept me for himself."

My stomach dropped at the implication. Jake muttered a curse under his breath.

"I had no choice," Sophia whispered. "Tony forced himself on me, again and again. And when I became pregnant, he took my baby from me as soon as she was born. My Anna. I was only 12 years old."

Tears streamed freely down Sophia's face now. My heart ached for the young girl she had been, abused and violated. For the mother robbed of her child.

"He let me go, but only after forcing me to take a blood oath of silence. If I ever breathed a word, Anna would pay the price." Sophia's voice hardened with quiet fury. "I left to try and build a life, always hoping I could find a way to get my daughter back. And now, with Michael here..."

She raised her eyes to us, rimmed red with heartbreak.

"Please. Help me save my Anna. He allowed me to see her a few times over the years. The last time I was allowed to see her I slipped her a prepaid phone. I add minutes to it every month. She calls me when she can, when it's safe. She hasn't called and the phone doesn't ring any longer. It goes straight to voicemail. Something is wrong."

Sophia then completely broke down. Years of pain and trauma pouring out of this woman was devastating to witness.

Beau is out of his seat and around to Sophia's side of the desk. He sits on the floor in front of her and pulls her down into his arms. Sophia doesn't fight it, she needs the comfort, the strength, the support he is offering.

"We will do whatever it takes," Rex vowed.

Beside me, Jake nodded. "You have our word."

Rex crossed his arms, eyes hard as flint. "The Moretti's have hurt too many people. It's time someone made them pay."

Beau sat with Sophia, gently rocking her. Whispering in her ear so only she could hear. This was a completely different side of Beau from the hard, gruff man I've come to know.

I see Rex and Jake give each other a look, their thoughts no doubt mirroring mine. The three of us leave Sophia's office to give them some privacy.

Once we reach the parking lot, Rex turns to me, "did you know about any of that?"

"No, I had no idea about any of it. I knew Anna was Michael's sister. She lived with us and was never allowed to have a job, but neither was I. She never said Sophia was her mom when she told me to come here and find her. Only that she managed the Ridge, she agreed to give me a job, and I could trust her."

Rex nodded as I spoke, seeming to try to take it all in.

Just then Jake's phone buzzed. He checked the screen, "Oh shit baby, your appointment, we gotta be leavin' if we are going to make it on time."

"Oh my god! I completely forgot with everything that just happened. I'm going to be a terrible mother, I'm already forgetting about the baby."

Rex's expression turned serious as he shook his head. "Trust me, once that little tyrant is here, there will be no forgetting. That kid won't let you. You'll be elbow deep in shit, throw up, and probably a couple things you can't remember what it is, or identify, or even really fucking care at that point. Don't you worry, lil' momma, forgetting will not be an option."

Jake laughed, "damn Rex, you're really sellin' this parenting thing."

"Brother, it's already sold. You two should sleep and fuck while you still can. That's what you can forget about. Once that kid is here, you won't remember the last time you got to do either."

Rex climbs on his bike and takes off with a wave. Jake helps me into the truck and then climbs in the drivers seat.

"Baby, we aren't forgetting about either of those."

I burst out laughing at the firm expression on Jake's face. "I'll see what I can do."

We arrived at the Mason Women's Health Clinic only minutes before my scheduled appointment time. We quickly walk in but my steps falter when I see Christie at the check-in counter. Her eyes light up when they land on Jake and it makes my blood boil.

"Well hey there Jakey. Long time no..." she started enthusiastically before catching my glare. She cleared her throat, turning her megawatt smile down a few notches.

"I mean, nice to see you again Jake. And you too Sarah."

I bit my tongue, refusing to dignify her overt familiarity with Jake. We were here for the baby after all.

The nurse called me back within a few minutes. I settled onto the exam table, muscles finally relaxing now that we had made it just in time. I laid back on the table as she asked. The nurse lifted the bottom of my shirt over my belly and pulled my pants down below. She tucked a towel into my pants to protect them from the gel.

"OK sweetheart, this gel might be a little cold, but it will warm up quick. I'm going to take a few minutes getting some measurements and pictures of baby, and then we can get to the fun stuff."

Jake gripped my hand as the technician spread the icy gel over my belly. Suddenly our baby appeared on the screen. The strong heartbeat filled the room and Jake whistled.

"That there is the next heavyweight UFC champ. Listen to that right hook!" he joked. I swatted his arm but couldn't contain my smile.

The tech spent about 10 minutes taking measurements. Then

finally she turned the screen and showed us a profile shot. She pointed out the little nose and mouth, then showed us a tiny leg and foot.

"Would you like to know the gender?"

"Yes!" We both replied in unison.

She pointed to the screen. "Congratulations mom and dad, you've got a healthy baby boy!"

Jake pumped his fist, a proud grin spreading across his face. "Ha! I knew it. Gonna have me a little linebacker."

I rolled my eyes but joyful tears blurred my vision as I gazed at our son's profile. Our precious boy, it seems more real now. After everything today, this happy milestone reminded me that even a sliver of light can shine through the dark.

The tech printed photos for us before sending us on our way. As we exited the scan room, Jake wrapped a protective hand around my swelling belly. We approached the front desk to schedule a follow up in a month. Christie's eyes zeroed in on Jake's hand placement immediately.

"Do you have a preferred day or time you would like to schedule your next appoint? Perhaps a time that would work better for you so the father could make it?" she snarked in my direction.

Jake bristled, straightening to his full imposing height. "I thought I made this clear last time, but I'll spell it out for you today, I AM the father. And I'll be at every single appointment for my son, and my woman, not that it's any of your god damn business. I suggest you stick to doing your job, because anything else is none of your concern."

Christie recoiled a bit under his stern gaze before mumbling an apology and handing me a card with my next visit. I couldn't resist a smug smile as we walked out. Our son may enter a rocky world soon, but he'd have his fearless father watching over him.

Walking to Jake's truck, I pause. "What do you think she meant by that, Jake? Why would she assume you're not the father?"

"I think she was trying to give you a hard time because she wanted more from me than I was ever willing to give her. Now you have everything she wanted, and more. Don't worry about it Darlin', it's just jealousy."

On the drive back to the Rebel Sons Compound, I couldn't tear my eyes from the ultrasound photos. My heart swelling each time I trace a tiny finger or toe. I felt so much love for him already, but also so much fear for him.

Jake reached over, giving my knee a supportive squeeze. "I know that look. You're thinking about Sophia again, aren't you?"

"I am. What happened to Sophia, she was so young. Then to have Anna ripped away from her. The life Anna was born into, the hate, the violence, it's all she's ever known. We both had terrible childhoods, Jake. I just want this baby to have a good life and be happy, to never feel any of the pain we've all had to face. I just want better for him."

As we were pulling up to the front gates of the compound, Jake pushed a button on a remote hanging on his visor. The gates opened long enough for us to pull through, and then closed behind us. Jake remained silent as we parked in front of his townhouse and made our way inside.

Once the front door closed Jake picked me up suddenly, hands cupping my ass, and carried me to the kitchen counter.

"Jake! What are you doing?"

He places his large hands on either side of my face. "Our son will have better. Darlin' he already has a better life than you or I did, and he's not even born yet. He's got a mom and a dad who love him, who would walk through fire for him. Who would sacrifice everything to ensure his happiness. That is better. Right outside this door, he's got eleven uncles, who would protect him with their lives. Not to mention Cass, Anna, Soph, and Gram. This little man has so much love for him already. Baby, our boy has better, and I promise you, I'll make sure it only keeps getting better for both of you."

"I love you so much Jake. I don't think I could have gotten through any of this without you."

Using his thumbs to wipe the tears from my cheeks, "yes you could have. You just wouldn't have enjoyed it as much."

Jake picks me up again, heading towards the back of the house.

"You know I can walk."

"I know babe, and I enjoy watchin' you walk from behind all the time. But right now, I can get us to our bed faster and that is where we need to be, naked."

Jake gently lowers me to my feet beside the bed and begins undressing me. He lifts my shirt up and over my head, letting it drop to the floor. With skillful fingers, he unclasps my bra and it slides down my arms until it falls to the floor between us.

I stand in front of Jake as he kisses my neck and leads me to the bed. He lays me down gently, and I let out a soft moan as his lips trail down my neck and across my chest. He pauses to caress one breast with his hand, taking my hardened nipple into his mouth and sucking hard while rolling the other between his thumb and finger.

"I love these tits Sarah, so perfect."

"Jake, that feels so good." I moan louder as he kisses his way down my stomach. I arch my back off the bed as wetness pools between my legs. "Jake please." I beg.

Jake smirks as he looks up at me from between my legs.

"Please what baby?"

"I need you, I want you inside of me. Jake, please, I need to feel you."

He chuckles as he licks my clit so agonizingly slow.

"I think you can wait a little longer."

I whimper in frustration, "Jake seriously, stop teasing me!"

He chuckles lowly, "want it bad, don't you baby? Be a good girl and I'll give you what you want." Jake continues to tease me with his mouth. Licking so slowly up and down my pussy. He nips lightly at my clit and the sensation makes my back arch and legs shake.

"Oh god, more, please." I feel him enter me with two fingers. His fingers curling up to find my g-spot, and I moan louder.

"That's it baby, let me hear you." He continues to bring me to the brink of orgasm, pausing right before I cum.

"You want my cock in your tight little pussy? You'll have me darlin', I promise. But first, I want to make sure you cum on my tongue."

He continues to work his magic with his mouth and fingers.

"Yes, Jake, don't stop!" I yell out as my orgasm washes over me.

Jake stands up and starts to remove his clothes. I can't help but watch as his shirt slides up over his broad shoulders and lands on the floor. His large hands unbutton his jeans, causing the muscles in his arms to flex as he slowly lowers the zipper down.

His pants fall down his thighs, freeing his erection. Fisting his cock, he slides his hand up and down his shaft.

"You like what you see?" Jake teases.

"You know I do." I whisper back, my voice still shaky from my orgasm. "I need you right now Jake, please."

"Get on your hands and knees baby."

I do as he says and feel him position himself behind me. He rubs the head of his hard cock through my wetness. Finally, he thrusts himself into me, filling me completely.

"Fuck, you feel good." He moans, thrusting in and out with deep, long strokes.

"Please don't stop." I beg as he pulls almost completely out, then plunges back in, even harder and deeper than before.

"Not a fucking chance," he growls as his thrusts get faster. I gripped the sheets in my hands, digging my nails in, as pleasure builds up inside of me again. Jake's grip on my hips tightens.

"You're so damn tight. You close? I need you to cum for me baby." He growls through gritted teeth.

"Yes, Jake, I'm gonna..." I couldn't finish my sentence as another orgasm rocks through me. Jake picks up the pace, slamming in and out of me until he comes inside of me with a hoarse yell.

"Jesus, fucking christ woman." He collapsed beside me, pulling me back into him, catching his breath. "I love you. You're mine, always been mine, Sarah, always will be." he panted.

"Always, I love you too Jake."

His reassuring warmth and the steady thump of his heart against my back lulled me toward sleep. But just as I start drifting off, I'm startled by Jake's voice.

"What do you think about the name Barrett?"

I rolled over to face him, suddenly wide awake. "For the baby?"

He nodded. "Yeah. Was thinking it sounds strong, you know? A badass name for a badass kid. Any kid of mine will naturally be a badass. So the name has to live up to the kid."

"I think it's perfect. Barrett Jacob Riggs."

"Jacob, really?" The surprise in his voice was evident.

"Absolutely, the name has to live up to the kid, right?"

Jake's face split into a grin before he pulled me in for a kiss. Our sweet boy had a name. Barrett. I nestled into Jake's arms and finally surrendered to sleep's pull, the future feeling a little less daunting.

CHAPTER 23

Jake

The blistering Montana sun beat down on me as I helped my brothers set up tables and a makeshift bar outside, behind the clubhouse. We were getting ready for the big 4th of July blowout tomorrow commemorating the 40th year of the Rebel Sons.

Jett wiped his brow as he climbed down from hanging lights. "Hey, did you give Sarah a heads up on what this party can get like?" he asked.

I paused, realization dawning on me that I hadn't properly prepared her for the chaos 10 visiting chapters of the Rebel Sons brings. "Ah shit, no I didn't even think about it."

Talon chuckled, clapping me on the back. "Well you know after the fireworks when the kids clear out, things tend to get a little wild once the whiskey flows free. Don't want our lil' momma getting spooked thinking we're a bunch of animals once the clothes start coming off."

"Yeah, good call. I doubt she's ever been around a pack of bikers in their natural habitat." I head into the clubhouse in search of Sarah. Jax finds me walking through the common room.

"Hey Jake, you got a second?"

"Yeah man, what's up?"

"I was just coming to find you and Beau. Wanted to let you know it's been all quiet on the Moretti front. The old man is still on the east coast. There has been no activity to track Michael, so it's still unconfirmed whether he is alive or not. His leave of absence with the DEA was extended from 6 months to 12 earlier this week. That's the only intel that's come in from all the monitoring alerts I have set up. No chatter within the organization either, completely quiet."

"Is that extension something he would have had to do in person?"

"No, it was a form that was filled out and sent back in with an email. So, no way of telling if it was Moretti, or someone sending it on his behalf."

I nod in understanding, "good job Jax. Keep it up. Let me know if anything changes."

Leaving Jax, I continue on my search for Sarah. I find her inside the blessedly air conditioned clubhouse kitchen, laughing with Gram as they prepped food for tomorrow. The heavenly scent of Gram's famous potato salad wafted through the air.

"Gram, please tell me your lettin' my girl in on the secret of how you make your potato salad."

"Absolutely dear, this one is a keeper. I've already shown her how to make my chocolate chip cookies and now my potato salad. She's gotta carry on my traditions to show your daughters and daughter in laws. And someone will have to take care of all my boys around the clubhouse one day when I'm gone. You got a good one in her Jake, I couldn't have picked anyone better."

Rex and X walk into the kitchen, X going right to Gram to give her a kiss on the cheek.

"Yeah Gram, Jake is one lucky bastard. Unfortunately for me, I can't say the same for myself. Any way I can get some of that potato salad? You're the only beautiful woman in my life that takes care of me and feeds me. You ever think about becoming an old lady again? You feed me every day, I could definitely knock the dust off and give you a hell of a ride."

Rex punches X in the shoulder, "You ever say some shit like that to my grandma again you won't have to worry about eating. You won't have any damn teeth left in your mouth."

"Fuck Rex, calm down. I was just playing." X winks at Gram and shakes his head behind Rex's back so only Gram can see.

Sarah, laughing at X's antics, "apparently I do need to learn everything I can from you Marlene. Gram's still got it going on."

"Damn straight." That comment earned X another punch to the arm from Rex.

I walk up behind Sarah, wrapping my arms around her waist. "Hey baby, can I borrow you for a minute?"

Her emerald, green eyes met mine, clearly sensing the tension in my voice. She excused herself and followed me into Beau's office.

"What's wrong?" she asked, worry etched into her face.

I sat down on the couch, pulling her down onto my lap.

"Hey now, nothing's wrong Darlin', just wanted to talk to you about tomorrow. I wanted to give you a heads up about what to expect tomorrow night. With 10 chapters all together, things can get a little crazy after the fireworks are over, and it's just us adults left."

Sarah smiled at me in understanding, "Jake, I already figured as much. You boys all seem to like your fun."

"Well, it's a little more than fun. It isn't exactly a church picnic once the sun goes down and the booze starts flowin'."

"How so?"

"Well for one, fights tend to break out when that much testosterone mixes with booze," I said with a wry grin.

"And some of the visiting chapters have...companions that travel with them."

Sarah's eyes widened as the realization set in. "You mean club girls?"

I nodded. "Yeah. Clothes tend to come off too, which I know you ain't use to."

Sarah raised one delicate brow. "You saying I should prepare myself to see you naked in public, Jake Riggs?" A teasing grin tugged at her lips.

I barked out a laugh. "Hell no, that's only for you, darlin'." I took her hands in mine. "I just don't want you feelin' uncomfortable or getting the wrong idea about me. Some of the club girls from other chapters can get a little... friendly. Even if it's not wanted. Our chapter never allowed that shit. My grandfather would have never disrespected Gram like that, and I'll never disrespect you like that. But the parties still get wild."

Sarah smiled, patting my cheek affectionately. "I appreciate the warning, babe. But I'm not some naive schoolgirl, I can handle it. I'm certain after living with Michael for 12 years, I don't think you bikers can do anything to surprise me."

I felt a protective rage well up inside me at the mention of her ex-husband that made me see red, but I tamped it down.

I pulled her in close. "I'm not planning on letting you out of my sight tomorrow night. If we would get separated, just know if anyone disrespects or touches you inappropriately you come find me, or one of my brothers. If it gets too much, you just say the word and we'll head home."

Sarah leaned in for a kiss. "My protector," she murmured against my lips. Sarah squeezed my calloused hands gently. "I appreciate the warning, but you don't have to worry about me. I know who you are, Jake. I love you, and a wild party won't change how much I trust you."

◆ ◆ ◆

By noon the next day, motorcycles were already arriving from chapters all over the country. Some came in large RV's, while others pitched tents on the open land. We manage to squeeze in about 75 people between the bunkhouse, empty apartments, and three vacant townhouses. However, even with that much space, it's never enough for our annual Fourth of July gathering. The area around the clubhouse transformed into a makeshift campground every year.

Sarah helped Gram and Cass carry out enough salads, bbq, and baked goods to feed a small army. Which was a good thing, since the crowd was massive by the time Beau stepped up to the mic for his speech right at sunset.

As darkness fell, Beau stepped up to the mic for his annual speech.

"We're here tonight to honor the tenacity and brotherhood of the founders who took a dream and turned it into all of this 40 years ago," Beau's voice boomed across the crowded field. He spoke reverently of his father's legacy and his grit and determination in building the club from the ground up.

On cue, Ranger stood and lifted his beer, his leathery face cracking into a grin. As president of the Canyon City chapter now, he and Beau's father had started all of this back in the day. Their shared history was legend among the club.

He raised his glass towards the white-haired man surrounded

by patched members. "Pops, Ox, and Ranger. You're the only originals left standing. We all thank you and respect you for paving the way for all of us. We've been through hell and back together over the years, but the ties that bind us are unbreakable."

Then Beau turned towards Sarah and me, beckoning us forward. My heart swelled with pride as we made our way through the sea of clapping bikers to stand before my uncle.

"We also have an exciting announcement this year. Tonight we also celebrate the continuation of our family, our legacy." Beau bellowed joyfully. "My nephew Jake has finally found his old lady. This gorgeous girl here is Sarah. They're expecting an addition to the Riggs clan!

The crowd erupted into raucous cheers and applause. I wrapped an arm around Sarah as she beamed up at me.

"A son to carry on the family name. Little Barrett Jacob will be the first of a new generation to uphold the brotherhood and traditions the originals started 40 years ago." More deafening cheers rose up.

Sarah wiped at the tears welling in her eyes. I knew she was touched deeply to be so openly welcomed into the family by the club. After a lifetime of loneliness, she had found her people.

We settled onto a blanket to enjoy the fireworks, Sarah nestled between my legs and encircled in my arms. The booms and crackles filled the sky, but all I could focus on was her. This remarkable woman who walked back into my life so unexpectedly. The mother of my child. My family.

"I never imagined I would find a family after everything I've been through," she murmured over the boom of bursting rockets. "I thought me, and this baby would be on our own, probably running for rest of my life. But being here with all of you, I feel like I'm really home. Thank you Jake. You've given me so much more than you even realize."

I'd been trying to find the perfect way to ask her to move in for weeks. Now seemed like the right time. I turned her to face me. Taking her hands in mine, I met her gaze.

"Sarah, I want you to have a real home. A place that's yours, just as much as it is mine, where you feel safe and happy."

Her eyes widened but she stayed silent, letting me continue.

"I know we never talked specifics, but will you move in permanently with me? I want us to really build a life together. A real home for you, me, and Barrett. Whatever you want, baby. We could fix up my trailer, or I could build us a house on my land. Or we can stay in the townhouse here on the compound now that you're part of the family. I just want us all together before Barrett gets here."

Her smile cut off my rambling. "Jake," she said softly, taking my face in her hands. "I would love nothing more than to make a home with you."

CHAPTER 24

Sarah

With no news on Michael, and no retaliation from the Moretti family, the last few months of my pregnancy passed quietly. Jake and I settled into domestic life together. We fall into a comfortable routine - going to work, coming home, cooking dinner together while chatting about our days. After cleaning up the kitchen, we curl up on the couch to relax, Jake's hand absently stroking my swollen belly as we watch TV.

I decided to stay in the cozy townhouse on the club compound, while we build a home near Jake's trailer behind the B&B. It will be nice staying near Marlene to have her help with Barrett initially. As a first-time mom, I love the idea of having Marlene close by incase I need her.

About a month before my due date, Jake and I spent the weekend decorating the nursery. We both agreed on a vehicle theme, reflecting Jake's love for cars and motorcycles. We adorned the walls with vintage hot rods, muscle cars, and choppers in a striking color scheme of red, black, and gray. I couldn't help but chuckle as Jake seemed even more enthusiastic about the decor than I was.

Beau has a passion for woodworking, and I have been lucky enough to see some of his work. He offered to make all the furniture for the nursery as a gift. Jake also lent a hand in the construction process. As I stand in the doorway of Barrett's room, I can't help but smile at the thought of rocking our baby to sleep in that beautifully crafted chair. It makes it so much more special that it was made by his dad and great uncle. Maybe one day Barrett will rock his children in it. It's moments like these that make me appreciate the kindness and support from my new family.

As my due date comes and goes, I grow anxious, but the doctor assures me it's common to go past it. At my last appointment, Dr. Turner says they'll induce me right at 42 weeks if I haven't gone into labor by then.

The Monday morning before Thanksgiving, when Jake is leaving for work, he walks me over to the clubhouse to spend the day baking with Marlene, Cass, and Emmalynn while he's at the garage.

Saying our goodbyes, I groan in relief when Jake cups my belly from the bottom, taking some of the pressure off my back and hips.

"Oh my god, I gotta get him out of me. I can't take this anymore."

X seems to come out of nowhere, popping up behind Jake's back.

"Hey now lil' momma, that's no way to talk about Jake. Don't be so hard on him, I'm sure he's trying his best. I can offer some advice if you'd like, give him a few pointers. Or we could just let him watch, and I can show him how it should be done."

Gram yell's out from the kitchen, "I thought I was your girl, X?"

"Oh babe, you're my number one girl, but lil' momma is sounding desperate. What kind of gentleman, or brother would I be if I left Jake's girl in need of relief when I have the skill set to make her feel good." X yelled back at the kitchen door.

"X, you even think about touching my woman, or Gram, and I'll beat your pretty boy face in." Jake's tone was playful, but he meant every word.

X couldn't stop laughing, "Rigg's men are such easy targets to fuck with. I used to date a girl who worked at a day spa; she taught me some massage techniques. I can show you how to ease some of that pressure on her back, sides, and hips that little man is putting on her."

"Oh Jake, please let him show you later after work, that sounds amazing. I'm so uncomfortable."

Jake gives X an angry glare, "Be here at 6:00. And don't make any comments about how you know what she likes or how you can do it better. Just...don't be your usual self. Keep the smart ass fuckery at a minimum."

"I don't even have to say it, brother. Just look at her smile. She knows my fuckery is top-notch." X grins and pats me on the back. "See you at 6:00, sweetheart. I'll bring some warming massage oil. Maybe I'll pick up one that will make you tingle, although we both know I won't need any help." X winks at me and heads out of the clubhouse through the front door.

"I really am miserable Jake."

"I know baby, a little bit longer. He'll either come when he's ready or we'll evict him next week. I gotta head out to open the garage. Call me if I need anything, no matter how small. I'll be home around 5:30." He kisses my forehead.

"Love you, Jake."

"Love you too darlin'."

A few hours after Jake leaves, Emmalynn and I are baking cookies in the kitchen. My back has been aching intensely all morning, and rolling out the dough for cut out cookies is making it worse. I wince, rubbing at the tightness in my hips. Beau and Wyatt stop by to check on us.

"Would one of you guys mind helping her roll out the rest of that dough. She does really well using the cookie cutters on her own. I just need to sit down for a few minutes and take a break."

"Sure thing lil' momma." Beau says as he's already walking around the counter towards his granddaughter.

"Look grandpa! I made turkeys and pumpkins! Sarah helped a little too." Emmalynn showed her grandpa proudly all the cookies we had made.

"I see that Em, they look great. I might eat a few before me and Wyatt head out in a bit."

"No grandpa, Gram said they are for Thanksgiving dinner. You don't get any yet."

As I'm slowly making my way to sit at the table, I feel a pop and suddenly fluid is gushing down my legs.

"Oh! I think my water just broke!" I gasp.

Wyatt's eyes go wide with alarm, "Gram, Cass, I need someone with a vagina to come in here and deal with this."

Beau rushes around the counter to grab my hand and arm, to lead me the rest of the way to the table to sit down.

"Christ Wyatt, you're the one acting like you have a vagina. Go get the club van and bring it around to the front door. Find Parker on the way and tell him he's got a mess to clean up in the kitchen." Beau orders, and Wyatt left the kitchen like his ass was on fire.

Marlene comes rushing into the kitchen and quickly takes charge, while Cass starts timing my contractions.

Parker comes into the kitchen, "hey Prez, Wyatt said you needed me."

"Yeah Park, Sarah's in labor and we need to get her to the hospital. Her water broke over there on the floor near the table. Go clean that up."

"For real Prez? I've never complained about anything before, but baby juice? Can't Cass clean it up?"

"You want a patch someday?" Parker nods. "That's what I thought, get a mop and stop whining like a little bitch." Then Beau's face softens as he turns towards me. "Come on lil' momma, let's get going so you can meet your little rebel. Or we could set you up right here in the kitchen and give Parker something to really bitch about cleaning up."

"Beau, as fun as torturing Parker sounds, I think I'll stick with the hospital."

"Suit yourself."

Beau and Cassandra carefully help me waddle out to the club van as contractions start coming harder.

"Sarah, do you have a hospital bag packed already?" Cass asked as she helped me into the back of the van.

"Yes, there are two bags on the floor of the closet in Barrett's room. A diaper bag for the baby and one for me."

Beau's voice booms, "Wyatt, go over to Jake's place and grab the two bags sitting on the floor of the closet in the baby's room. Help Gram watch Emmalynn until you get ahold of Rex, then one of you bring the bags to the hospital."

I call Jake in between contractions once we're on the road, keeping my voice as calm as I can when he answers.

"Hey Beautiful."

"Hey babe, are you busy?"

"It's fine Sarah, are you OK? What's wrong?"

"I'm fine Jake. It's just that I was making cookies with Emmalynn and my water kind of broke. So, if you're not too busy right now, I think it's time to leave for the hospital."

"For fuck sake Sarah, you're in labor and you start off with, 'Hey babe, are you busy?'!"

Beau laughs out loud from the seat next to me, clearly amused by Jake's irritation towards me.

"I'm getting on my bike now, do NOT push until I get there. I'll be right behind you."

"I'll try daddy, no promises."

"Sarah, I love you, but keep your damn legs crossed till I get there."

Another contraction cuts off my laughter at Jake. "Love you too, gotta go." Then I end the call, handing my phone off to Beau."

Cass coaches me through breathing techniques as well as she can while driving, as Beau holds my hand. We pull up to the hospital entrance and Beau helps me out of the van while nurses get me settled into a wheelchair. I'm taken straight to labor and delivery while we wait for Jake to arrive.

Jake comes bursting into the room, panic etched on his face until he sees me and knows I'm alright. Dr. Turner enters right behind Jake.

"Sarah and Jake, it looks like today is the big day. Sarah, I need to do a quick check to see how dilated you are." After a brief pelvic exam, she confirms, "You're currently at 5 cm, so you're halfway there. If you'd like, you can request an epidural at this point. It will probably be a few more hours until you reach 10 cm. I know in the office you mentioned you were wanting a natural birth. The choice is completely up to you."

"Dr. Turner, I didn't know what the hell I was talking about. I'll take the epidural, make it a double."

With an amused smile, "Two won't be necessary Sarah. I think you'll get a lot of relief with just one. I'll put the orders in now, and send the anesthesiologist in.

A few minutes pass before the anesthesiologist enters the room. Jake keeps a close eye on him, looking concerned at the sight of the large needle that is about to be inserted into my back. "Are you sure that's the right size, doc?" he asks anxiously.

"Mr. Riggs, trust me. I've done this a million times, I won't hurt her," the doctor assures him.

As the epidural takes effect, I feel my body relaxing, the pain dulling as a warmth spreads through me. After that I'm able to rest more comfortably until I'm fully dilated and ready to push. Jake grabs my hand encouragingly and I bear down with all my might as the doctor counts for me. I feel the baby descend lower with each push.

Jake takes my hand in his, his grip firm but reassuring as he tells me, "You're doing amazing, baby." With a final agonizing push, our baby slips out into the doctor's waiting hands. Jake cuts the umbilical cord with an emotional smile as they place our wailing, tomato-red newborn on my chest.

We gaze in awe and joy at our son, Barrett Jacob Riggs, meeting him for the first time. After the nurses clean him up, they carefully lay Barrett in my arms. He roots around hungrily and latches on as I try to nurse him for the first time. Jake sits next to us on the bed, staring at our son in wonder, tears pooling in his eyes. He gently strokes Barrett's downy head.

"Hey there, Barrett. I'm your daddy. And I promise to always be here for you." His voice cracks with emotion. Overwhelmed with love, I think how this perfect child has made our family complete.

Once I'm settled, Jake climbs into the narrow hospital bed with me, both of us blissfully cradling our son, cherishing these first precious moments as a family.

On Thanksgiving Day, Barrett and I are discharged from the

hospital. As we drive from Mason toward the Rebel Sons compound, bundles of nerves and excitement churn inside me. Jake grins at me, "ready for Barrett to meet the whole family?"

Marlene has prepared a wonderful Thanksgiving dinner for the whole club. Jake tenderly takes Barrett from his car seat and introduces our newborn son to everyone before dinner, beaming with pride.

"Everyone, I'd like you to meet the newest member of the Rebel Sons...Barrett Jacob Riggs.

I've never felt more thankful than in this moment, surrounded by family. My painful past no longer matters because my future with Barrett, Jake, and the new family I've found here is everything I've always hoped for.

CHAPTER 25

Jake

I arrive at the garage two hours early, irritated that I can't take Sarah to her postpartum checkup. I found out yesterday the parts order for the week was all wrong. If I don't get this fixed and the right parts delivered today, it'll put us behind schedule on two custom builds.

Cass offered to go with Sarah to Mason to help wrangle Barrett so I can try to sort out this mess at the shop. I had one of our prospects, Dom, follow behind them to the clinic just to keep an eye on them and make sure they get there and back safely. I'm on hold with the parts supplier trying to fix the order when Jax calls. I debate not answering to stay focused on the parts issue but something tells me I better see what he needs.

"Jake, we got a big fucking problem," Jax says urgently.

My stomach drops. "What's going on?"

"Dom was waiting outside the clinic for Sarah and Cass to be done with the appointment," he explains. "But while he was parked out front, two black SUVs came speeding out of the rear lot. Dom went inside to find them, but Sarah and Cass were gone."

"Gone?" My stomach drops. "What do you mean gone?" The panic was rising inside of me.

"I hacked into the clinic's security system," Jax continues. "Right after Sarah checked in at the front desk, one of the nurses let three armed guys in through a back entrance. They were in and out in under two minutes with Sarah, Cass and the baby, then peeled out in those SUVs."

I grip the phone tightly, mind racing. "Did you get eyes on them after they left?"

"I picked them up on traffic cameras heading out of town," he confirms. "Took Route 8, so they are either heading toward North Ridge or I-90. Prez already sent Dom in the direction of I-90, to see if he can catch up to them if they went that way. Prez and a few others are riding out Route 8 now to head them off if they are coming this way."

My jaw clenches with rage. "It's gotta be that psychotic bastard Moretti. Text me any footage you pulled and alert the others. I'm headed to the clubhouse now."

I burst out of my office, yelling for X, Wyatt and Rex who are all with me at the garage today. "Sarah, Cass, and my son were just grabbed. We need to get to the clubhouse now!"

We all climb onto our bikes and speed towards the Rebel Sons compound. Beau, Jett, Gunnar, and Patch have just returned, unsuccessful in their search on Route 8. My hands clench into fists at my sides, consumed with a desire to mercilessly kill the fucker responsible for taking my family away from me.

We gather in the chapel to wait anxiously for any update from Dom. Jax comes in and sets up the TV in the chapel to play the security footage he pulled from the clinic in Mason. It starts and I watch as a door at the rear of the building opens. The female employee steps out of the way to allow the three armed men entry. She turns her face towards the camera as she does.

"It's Christie. That fucking cunt. How in the hell did she get involved with Moretti?" I roar in frustration.

"Who the fuck is Christie?" Wyatt asks, clearly confused.

"Someone I should have known better than to stick my dick into." I yell, pissed off at myself more than anyone else.

Rex stops me from leaving the room. "This isn't your fault Jake. How the hell could you have known the bitch would turn out to be nuttier than squirrel shit?"

Beau's phone rings, "it's Dom." Beau answers the phone on speaker. "What did you find, Dom?"

"I never caught up to the SUVs before hitting the I-90. I was hauling ass to try to catch up and nothing. So, I was trying to think of somewhere they could have pulled off. The only place to turn off is that small private airstrip. That's where I'm at now. The two SUVs are here but they're long gone. Jake, I'm sorry I couldn't get to them in time, man. I tried."

Beau starts to speak but is interrupted by Jax who is already typing furiously on his keyboard. "I'm already on it Prez," Jax says with determination.

"Dom get back to the clubhouse as fast as you can. Good work, checking the airstrip." Beau ends the call.

"Boys, I think Dom just earned his patch. Flight logs confirm there was a small carrier plane that departed Brighton airstrip 10 minutes ago. The name on the flight log is Bruno Capparelli. He's the lowlife running the chop shop Moretti runs their west coast operations out of. The destination is listed as Portland." Jax then pulls up a video clip taken at the airport. It shows the three armed men pushing Cassandra, and Sarah holding Barrett into the plane. Christie followed in behind them.

Beau starts barking orders, "Brothers, grab your bags and get ready to ride, we are heading' out to Portland to get our girls and little rebel back. We'll leave within the hour.

Talon, plan the route, and call any clubs whose territory we will be riding through and give them a heads up.

X, call the Presidents of the Tacoma and Trinidad chapters. They are the closest chapters to Portland. I want as many men as they can spare sent to Portland to provide us support.

Rex, call the Canyon City, Durango, and Dumas chapters. Put them on standby, tell them we won't know if, or how many men are needed until we get more intel on what Moretti's numbers look like.

Pops and Ox, keep an eye on Marlene and Emmalynn. Don't leave the compound unless necessary. I'll call Sophia, I'm going to have her stay here at the compound. Show her which townhouse is mine when she gets here, she can stay there. I'll let her know. I want her here when we bring her daughter home to her.

Park, get the club van. Make sure it's ready to go, your driving. Every knows what they are doing. Go handle your shit and be ready to go in 45 minutes."

My jaw tightens, thinking of my sister, an innocent bystander. Picturing Sarah terrified and clutching Barrett to her chest. If that sick freak so much as lays a finger on them, I swear I'll rip him apart, limb by limb, with my bare hands.

Within the hour, we've got the bikes loaded up and are rumbling out of the compound, the roar of our engines echoing my simmering rage. We press on mile after mile through the night, hellbent on returning with my sister, Sarah, and my boy safe.

We rolled into a truck stop just outside Portland at dawn, greeted by a couple dozen Tacoma and Trinidad riders who came to provide support. Now we just need to pinpoint where Moretti has them stashed. Jax starts digging into all of Moretti's real estate holdings and business associates in the area, searching for any properties he could use.

One promising lead emerges, in Jax's research into Michael, he remembered an abandoned boatyard Moretti allegedly uses to load the girls being sent to Mexico into shipping containers. It could be our best shot at picking up the trail. Jax finds the address and we all roll out towards the coast.

We quietly surround the boatyard and spread out to cover all the exits. Scanning the rows of shipping containers, I finally spot a black SUV with dark tinted windows backed into one corner. This has gotta be it.

My heart starts hammering against my ribs. I signal the others to start closing in. As we converge on the SUV, the driver's door abruptly swings open. It's not Moretti, just one of his thugs.

The man freezes like a deer in headlights at the sight of a dozen guns aimed at him. "Hands up, dickbag!" Rex barks.

I holster my SIG and stride over to grab a fistful of the guy's shirt, slamming him up against the side of the vehicle.

"Where the hell are they?" I snarl through clenched teeth, my forearm crushing his windpipe.

The thug's eyes go wide with fear. "I dunno who you mean, man!" he wheezes.

I slam him against the SUV again, hard. "The two women and the baby you helped kidnap! Now tell me where they are before I put a bullet in your fucking skull!"

Gasping for breath, he confesses in a panic, "South warehouse! We were just hired to transport them, I swear!"

I hurl him to the ground and take off sprinting for the south warehouse, Beau right on my heels. Throwing open the door, we find Cassandra bound inside, roughed up but alive. No sign of Sarah or Barrett.

I cut Cass free of her restraints and grab her shoulders. "Are you OK Cass?"

"I'm OK now. I was so scared Jake. I'm so glad you're here." She throws herself at me so hard it knocks me back on my ass from my crouching position beside her.

"You're safe now Cass. We got you. I need to find Sarah and Barrett. Do you know where they are?"

She shakes her head, sobbing harder than before. "I don't know! They split us up after we got off the plane. I went in one SUV, and Sarah and the baby were put in another. I did hear the driver of the other SUV tell the guy who brought me here they had to make a stop at Bruno's. He was to keep me here to load me on one of the shipping containers."

"Motherfucker!" I throw the metal folding chair that sits in the middle of the warehouse against the wall. I'm too pissed off and scared I'll never see my family again to keep myself together.

X enters the warehouse and rushes over to my sister, "Cassandra!" He embraces her tightly and she clings onto him, seeking comfort. X speaks softly to Cass, so only she can hear, as he holds her close. His words seem to have a calming effect on her. We follow X as he carries Cass out of the warehouse, with Beau and I trailing behind them.

I make my way back to the SUV where Ridge, our Tacoma President, has taken charge. He's resorted to roughing up the thug to extract a location from him. After some convincing, he confirms what Cass overheard. They were taken to Bruno Capparelli's chop shop and are being held in cells in the basement.

I quickly glance back to confirm that X has Cass safely inside the van, out of sight from what's about to unfold. I calmly aim my gun, I pull the trigger and put a bullet through the man's skull. There are at least tow more who will meet the same fate today for taking my family from me. And one more for sending them to take what's mine. Retribution.

Ridge leaves two prospects from the Tacoma chapter to clean up.

The rest of us climb on our bikes and race to get towards the chop shop, each mile feeling longer than the last. All I can do is plead over and over in my mind for Sarah and Barrett to hold on, that I'm coming for them.

We park our bikes a couple blocks away from the chop shop so they don't hear us coming. We split up in two groups, one group to enter the front and one to enter the back. We scope out the place for a few minutes before we go in.

I get a text from Patch that there are two armed guards inside a fenced area at the back of the shop. The front is all clear except a security camera pointing at the front entrance.

"Jax, can you cut the power to the building? Turn it off long enough for us all to get in place. Then back on when we gain entry." I point the camera out to him.

"Sure thing boss, I'll have it down within a few minutes. I'll give you the all clear when it's safe to move in."

Less than two minutes later Jax has the power cut to the building. Wolf, the President of the Trinidad chapter, and Ridge, are leading their men into the back of the building. I'm leading my guys in through the front. I hear Wolf whistle, signaling the two guards in the back are taken care of and it's a go to enter.

At Beau's signal, we smash through the door and burst in, firing controlled pairs at the two muscle heads inside. They dive for cover behind the car in the garage bay they were working on, shouting in alarm and shooting back wildly. My pulse thrums as adrenaline takes over. I charge forward, pumping round after round into both men until the threats are neutralized.

With Rex covering me, I quickly clear the rest of the shop. No Sarah. No Barrett. Beau grips my shoulder firmly, seeing the torment and panic rising in my eyes. "We have to check the basement, son. I feel it, they are here."

We find the door to the basement inside an office. We cautiously descend the stairs. There is a group of men playing cards at a table. When they spot us they raise their weapons but are too slow. Rex and I take out all four men before they even get a shot off.

As we quietly approach the hallway leading to rooms in the back, I hear a small cry. *Barrett.* It's the best fucking sound I've ever heard in my life. Overwhelming relief crashes over me.

Then I hear his voice, Michael. They didn't hear the sounds of our gun shots because of our silencers. I approach the doorway to the room they are in. The door is closed but I can see into the room through the small window in the door.

Michael looms over Sarah, who is sprawled on the ground. Her lip is split open and bleeding, but I can't see any other injuries from where I stand. With malice in his words, he slowly unbuckles his belt as he continues to spew hatred at her.

"You actually thought you could escape me? Take my son and think I would let that happen? You're a foolish cunt, Sarah. That boy in the other room is the heir to the Moretti empire. My son, my flesh and blood. He will be raised by me and taught how to properly lead our family. One day, he will control both east and west coasts. Allowing another man to lay claim to my son. You insolent fucking bitch! I'll find him and slit his throat after I slit yours. But first, I'll record myself fucking every single one of your holes and send it to Jake, so he knows exactly how his old lady died. Just as she lived, as my dirty little whore."

The fury raging through my body couldn't be contained any longer. I kicked the door in, a growl escaping me as I advanced on him. I'm on him before he even has time to reach for his weapon. I crushed his body against the wall with all my force and put my forearm into his throat crushing his airway.

"What the fuck were you planning to do with that belt Mikey? Planning to beat her with it until your lashes break her skin? Is that what really gets you off? How would you like it if the tables were turned?"

I bring the handle of my pistol down hard against his temple and he falls to the floor. I yell for Rex and ask him to cut his shirt and pants off him. A confused look passes Rex's face but he does what I ask without question. I grab the belt off the floor that Michael had dropped when I came into the room. I wrap the leather a few times around my hand, and with the buckle end, start whipping him with his own belt. The belt that he enjoyed beating Sarah with.

Michael's anguished cries echo throughout the room, and I know Sarah must be witnessing this. But I can't stop, I won't stop. She needs to know it's all over now. He will never lay a hand on her or anyone else again. She needs to see the truth: he was weaker than she ever was. The belt slices through the air repeatedly, leaving bloody marks with each strike against his skin. As his body begins to break under the lashes, his blood splatters across the room in droplets. When my arms grow tired, I finally kneel down to meet his barely open eyes.

"This is only a small taste of what you did to her for years. I should keep you alive to do this again and again, over and over just as you did to her. Sarah and my son need this to be over, for you to die. So that's what I'll give them. The bullet I'm goin' to put between your eyes isn't to end your pain, it's to put an end to hers. I'm going to give her that and everything else you were never man enough to give her."

I stand and put two rounds in the fucker's head and deliver Sarah's retribution.

I drop to my knees and pull Sarah into my arms, cradling her as small whimpers escape her lips as she clings to me like a lifeline. Then she suddenly snaps her head up, "Barrett, we have to get Barrett! I don't know where he took him, or where he had the men take Cassandra!"

"Don't worry lil' momma, he's right here. Uncle Beau has him, isn't that right little rebel. I'm going to take him out to the van, let Patch take a look at him. From what I can see, he's no worse for wear. He's a Riggs man, he's made of tough stuff. We already found Cass, don't worry about her. She's safe. You let Jake get you sorted sweetheart, and we'll be waiting for you outside." I turn to see Beau standing in the doorway, cradling Barrett protectively in his arms.

Sarah cries harder in relief at the sight of our son safely sleeping in Beau's arms. "Thank you, Beau." He nods at Sarah and leaves the room.

"Are you hurt Sarah?" I ask the question I'm not sure I'm strong enough to hear the answer to. I have no idea how much time Moretti had with her. What he could have done to her.

"Jake, I'm okay. Michael arrived about 20 minutes ago and took Barrett from me. He disappeared into another room for most of the time he was here. I only saw him for a few minutes before you came in. He hit me a couple times, but that's it. I need to leave this place and go back home. I want to be with our family."

"Alright baby, let's get you and our boy home."

As I help Sarah to her feet and we start making our way towards the door, a loud noise echoes from the hallway. We see Rex sprinting by, carrying a half-naked woman who is wrapped in his kutte. Sarah gasps next to me and quickly covers her mouth with her free hand.

"Oh my god, Anna!" Sarah yells and is out the door right on Rex's heels.

"I can't stop lil' momma, she's in a bad way. I gotta get her out to Patch so he can start working on her." His voice has a level of concern that I know isn't good. He's afraid she isn't going to make it.

We follow Rex out of the chop shop and halfway down the block to the parked van. Once he lays Anna down in the back, Sarah and I finally get a look at her. Her injuries are horrific.

"Patch you gotta help her man, it's bad. This is Soph's daughter and we gotta bring her back alive." Rex is already climbing into the back of the van beside Anna, holding her hand tightly.

The sobs leaving Sarah's body are gut wrenching. "We have to help her, Jake. She's the only reason I'm alive."

While Patch gets to work he reassures Sarah without taking his focus off Anna. "Sarah, I'm going to do everything I can for her, I promise you. We need to move now. I'll work on getting her stable but she needs a hospital with more equipment than I have in these bags."

Sarah climbs in the middle row of the van with Beau and Barrett.

"Baby I'm going to be right behind you. My bike is a couple blocks over. I'll be two minutes behind you at the hospital." I give Sarah a kiss and quickly rub a finger over Barrett's cheek then slide the door closed.

The van takes off down the street, and Wolf claps me on the shoulder. "I already had one of my prospects get your bike, it's across the street. I'll have them grab Beau and Rex's and bring them to the hospital. We'll get this all cleaned up, brother."

I give Wolf a slap on the back as I'm already taking off across the street. "Thank you, brother. Let everyone else know how much I appreciate everything you've all done. You ever need anything, I'm there."

"I already know it brother, no need to say it. Just go get that family of yours back where they belong. That's all the thanks we need."

CHAPTER 26

Sarah

I spent the next two weeks at Anna's bedside in a Portland hospital as she recovered from her injuries. Her wounds were extensive - lacerations along her torso, broken ribs, facial fractures, and broken fingers. But even worse was the damage Michael had inflicted on her mind. She refused to speak of what happened in that basement, shutting down or changing the subject anytime it was brought up. The only time I saw a spark of life return to Anna's eyes was when I brought Barrett in to visit her. His sweet coos and wide-eyed wonder seemed to pull her out of whatever prison she is locked in inside her mind.

Beau decided not to inform Sophia of the full extent of Anna's injuries yet. Anna had pleaded with us not to allow her mother to see her so battered and broken. She needed time to heal more before facing Sophia. My heart ached at keeping such a secret, but I respected Anna's wishes.

Anna and Rex seemed to form a strong bond during her recovery. He barely left her side, staying to support her even when the rest of us had to take a break. Anna seemed to take comfort in Rex's quiet, steady presence at her bedside. Rex and I alternated nights staying at the hospital with her. On the evenings when Rex went back to the hotel to sleep, he would arrive first thing in the morning as soon as visiting hours began, with coffee and pastries in hand. He'd sit reading out loud or playing cards to pass the time, keeping Anna company. Seeing the tender way he cares for her makes me think there could be something more between them than friendship, one day. Rex has suffered his own share of tragedy and loss. Perhaps they could find healing together. Jake noticed the change in his cousin too, giving me knowing glances when Rex rushed off to the hospital each day.

Once Anna's infections finally came under control and started clearing up, she slowly began getting stronger. Her appetite returned, along with some color in her pallid cheeks. After two long weeks, the doctors finally agreed she could be discharged and continue recovering at home.

The club had left the van for us to drive back to Montana. Parker got to ride Jake's bike home, though not without explicit threats of bodily harm if he damaged the bike in any way.

The morning of Anna's discharge, we piled into the van. As we pulled away from the hospital, she grasped my hand tightly. "Let's go home," she whispered. I squeezed back, my heart lifting.

"Should we stop at the house so you can pack up your things?" I asked Anna. She nodded silently.

We drove to the house Michael and I had shared outside of Portland, so Anna could pack up her belongings. For the first time, staring out the outside of the house, it really hit me that I was free now. Michael was never coming back here. Anna, Barrett, and I would never have to run or live in fear again. We could build a beautiful new life in North Ridge.

The empty house already felt foreign as we walked through the front door. The emptiness and quiet were almost eerie. Jake trailed behind us, tension evident in his broad shoulders. I could tell Jake felt uncomfortable being in the house that held such dark memories for me. I didn't blame him one bit, I couldn't stand it either. The whole place made my skin crawl now. I want nothing more than to pack up Anna's things quickly and get out of here.

Rex searches the house, taking anything from Michael's home office he thinks might provide useful intel on the trafficking ring. All the chapters of the Rebel Sons voted to work together to take down the trafficking ring after Cassandra, Barrett, and I were taken.

I decide to go upstairs to my old bedroom to see if any of my old clothes or belongings are still there or even worth taking. As I set Barrett's car seat on the floor, I heard a faint scuffling sound coming from the closet. I put a finger to my lips as Jake entered the room, then pointed to the closet. He drew his gun silently.

Throwing open the door, we found Christie cowering inside. Tears streamed down her face as she begged Jake not to hurt her.

"Jakey, I'm sorry. He told me he just wanted to meet his son and get to know him. He said his ex had cheated on him with you and kept him away from their child. I didn't think it was right, Jakey. You know what a good person I am. I couldn't turn my back on someone in need. He said all I had to do was let him know when the kid was born and when her appointments would be. He promised to bring me to Portland so we could be together and start a new life. I had no idea he would kidnap your sister, I swear. His men were only supposed to take the fat bitch and her kid, not anyone else. After we arrived in Portland, one of his men brought me here and I haven't seen anyone since. Please, Jakey, take me home. I have no money or transportation, I'm stuck here."

"Jake, can you come out here for a moment?" I waited until he was safely out of the way before closing the door behind him. On the outside of this door, Michael had installed two locks, one at the top and one at the bottom. I slid both locks into place and secured them with two padlocks, just like Michael had once done to trap me inside.

I turn to Jake, "There's nothing of value to me in that closet; it's all trash." I grab Barrett's car seat and exit the bedroom. I leave Christie behind along with my old life, without so much as a backwards glance.

I only get a few steps into the hallway when Jake grabs my hand to turn me around. "Darlin' you don't have to talk about it now. We don't have to talk about it this week, this month, or even this year. But one day when you're ready, we will talk about that closet and why there are two locks on the outside of that door."

Over the next few weeks, life started slowly returning to our new normal. I still hadn't gone back to work yet, I wanted a few more months with Barrett before I left him that long. It also meant I could be with Anna while Sophia was working at the Ridge. Beau was kind enough to let Sophia and Anna move into one of the vacant townhouses. Having her own space while staying close seems to be helping Anna transition back to daily life.

Anna continued her recovery, a sense of peace and light slowly returning to her eyes. She seems to grow more attached to Barrett each day. Bonding with her nephew seemed therapeutic for her wounded soul. She'd rock and sing to him for hours.

A swell of gratitude fills my heart as I take in the family that surrounds me now. The darkness that once enveloped us is finally fading away, and we can all move forward together.

EPILOGUE

Jake

Just before Barrett's first birthday, the house I've been building for my family is finally finished. It's a beautiful log cabin tucked back in the woods about a quarter mile behind my trailer and the B&B. I've worked on it in my spare time over the past year, wanting to surprise Sarah.

She hasn't seen the inside yet since I just put the finishing details on it.

I asked Anna if she could watch Barrett overnight so I can show the house to Sarah properly. She thinks we're just swinging by quickly so I can show her the finished product. Little does she know this is going to be so much more.

I pick Sarah up on my bike and we take the long gravel driveway back to the secluded cabin. When we pull up, I hear her small gasp of surprise taking in the size of it. This place is easily five times bigger than the small cottage we originally planned.

Over the past months I expanded the designs, wanting to give Sarah and our family room to really spread out and grow. I added extra bedrooms, bathrooms, a larger kitchen and family room, the works.

Sarah gives me a puzzled look as we walk inside the expansive great room. "This is huge, Jake! What happened to our cozy little cabin in the woods?"

I grin and pull her close. "I want us to have space for the future, room for our family. I'm hoping you'll give me a few more rugrats to fill it up."

Sarah smiles up at me, eyes misty. "It's perfect. Thank you for doing this for us."

I give her a full tour of the place, showing off all the living spaces, the large open kitchen with an island Barrett can sit at while she cooks, multiple bedrooms upstairs that I hope will someday hold our children.

Finally, I bring her downstairs to the master suite I designed just for us. Our big king size mattress sits alone in the middle of the room, waiting for Sarah to decorate it how she wishes.

She turns slowly, taking in the vaulted ceiling and large windows looking out into the woods behind the house. I watch her closely, waiting for the moment I know is coming.

Right on cue, Sarah turns back around to face me. And there I am, already down on one knee holding open the little black ring box I've had hidden in this house for months.

Sarah's green eyes go wide, hands flying up to cover her mouth in happy shock. I just grinned at her.

"You walkin' back into my life was the best thing that ever happened to me, aside from the day we met," I begin.

"You've given me this amazing family I never thought I'd have. Our boy Barrett... he's everything to me. But if you haven't noticed, I'm kind of a greedy bastard when it comes to you baby."

Sarah laughs through the tears starting to fall. I forge on, pouring my heart out.

"I want it all with you, Sarah. I want a wife to build a life and home with. I want more babies to fill up this big house I built for our family. I want to give you and our kids everything we never had but deserved. At eighteen, I knew you were the one for me. No one after you ever compared. Because if they couldn't make me feel the way you did, I refused to settle for less than that. You're it for me, Sarah. You have been all along."

I pause, taking the ring out of the box. The glittering princess cut solitaire I picked out. Simple but stunning, just like my Sarah.

"So what do you say, Darlin'? You doin' this with me." I hold my breath waiting for her answer.

Sarah pulls me to my feet and crashes into my arms, half laughing, half sobbing. "Yes, yes of course I'm doing this with you!"

Grasping Sarah in my arms, I twirl her around and draw her close for a passionate kiss. As we pull away, our foreheads touch and we both cannot stop smiling. Carefully, I slide the diamond ring onto her finger.

Sarah holds out her hand, admiring the way the ring catches the light. "It's so beautiful, I love it." She looks up at me adoringly. "I love you. I can't wait to be your wife."

A surge of desire courses through me looking into her sparkling eyes. I scoop Sarah into my arms again. "I think we need to properly christen our new house, don't you?"

Sarah responds by crashing her lips to mine again. I carry her further into the bedroom and lay her gently down on the plush mattress.

My hands glide beneath her shirt, peeling it off slowly to reveal her creamy expanse of tantalizing skin. I trail kisses from the hollow of her throat, down between the valley of her breasts, making her shiver under me.

Sarah moans and arches her body up into mine as I suck her soft, rosy nipple into my mouth. Her nipples harden under my tongue's attention. I begin to kiss my way down her stomach, teasing her thighs. I slowly trace my fingers down the contours of her body, dancing over the fabric of her soaked panties. The scent of her arousal lights a fire within me - a primal growl rumbling deep in my chest as I slide them down, off her legs.

I dive in eagerly, running my tongue along every inch of her glistening folds, relishing in the taste of her sweetness. She gasps loudly when I find her clit, my tongue swirling around it with just the right amount of pressure that she loves, until she cries out in pleasure. Every gasp and whimper she releases against my working mouth drives my desire for her even further.

My fingers slide easily inside her pussy. Her tight warmth clenched around them like a vice. "You're so fucking tight and wet for me."

She grips my hair and pushes herself further onto my face, craving more as I take her completely into my mouth; tasting every inch of her sweetness. One of Sarah's hands fist in my hair guiding me closer to her release. Her hips buck wildly when she finds it; a climax rocks through her body as she cries out my name.

"Jake! Jake," she pants between breaths, "Please...I need you inside me."

I stand to take my pants off. When they fall to the floor my cock springs free. Sarah surprises me coming up off the mattress and licking my entire length from base to tip. Then she slid her wet mouth down my entire length, her tongue tracing the contours of my cock until I felt myself hit the back of her throat. Her bright green eyes never left mine, as I struggled to maintain control.

"Fuck baby... Sarah, it's too fucking good. You gotta stop." Sarah slides off me with a smirk, and lies back down on the bed.

I climb on the mattress, covering her beautiful body with mine, and slowly slide into her, inch by inch. Our eyes locked on one another. I want to go slow but the feel of her pussy squeezing around my dick has my control slipping. I slide out until just the tip is still inside of her before slamming back in, groaning as she screams my name. Picking up speed, I grip her hips tighter, driving in harder, sweat coating both our bodies.

"Jake, I'm so close, it feels so good."

"Give me another one Sarah," trying to hold off but I'm so close. When her pussy starts spasming around me with her own orgasm, I find my release deep within her. Collapsing onto the bed beside her gasping for air; Sarah cuddles against my side running soothing hands over my back and chest as we both come down from our orgasms. We lay together tangled in the sheets, Sarah's head pillowed on my chest as I stroked her silky hair.

We eventually get up and dress, I need to show her one last thing. Out on the back porch, I show Sarah the large wooden swing I built for her looking out over the surrounding woods.

We sit together gazing up at the stars, Sarah's head nestled perfectly on my shoulder. I wrap an arm around her and make quiet promises about our future. "I meant what I said," I murmured. "I'm going to give you and our family an amazing life, Sarah. Our kids will have better, but Darlin', we're gonna have better too."

Printed in Great Britain
by Amazon